## "Marry me, Jamie. Tonight."

Everything inside Jamie screamed for her to say yes. But her practical side cautioned her to proceed carefully. She and Kell had tried to be toge— very much, Kell. Bu—

"Why no— arms and trailed s— collarbone.

Jamie melted. "Kell, you aren't being fair. I can't think with you pressed this close to me."

He lifted his head and looked deeply into her eyes. "I like being pressed close to you. As you can feel, I want to make love to you. Here. On the beach."

"My, my, you are impetuous tonight. First you want to marry me, then you want to make love to me—all in the same night."

Kell pulled back. The bright moonlight illuminated the look of bemusement on his face. "Well, that's the right sequence, isn't it? First comes love, then comes marriage, then comes making love on a moonlit beach..."

"I think you forgot the baby carriage."

Kell pulled her down to the sand. "Not without the making love part first..."

Dear Reader,

How many times have you heard couples say..."We were high school sweethearts"? Or, "I've known him since we were kids"? For many, this isn't a fantasy, but a wonderful reality. They got it right the first time.

But that doesn't happen often. And I got to wondering... would these people have fallen in love if they'd met again when they were older? Would the same chemistry be there? Hard to know, isn't it?

In my first Temptation, *Her Only Chance*, I got to explore these possibilities. Jamie is a child of divorce and seeks security. Kell is a Navy SEAL, used to risking his life but not his heart. They have tremendous passion for each other—and share just as many problems. They can't be together—yet they can't stay apart. Neither one is willing to throw away all the love and the history they've shared.

Do they stand a chance? Read on and find out....

Enjoy,

Cheryl Anne Porter

# Books by Cheryl Anne Porter

**HARLEQUIN DUETS**
12—PUPPY LOVE
21—DRIVE-BY DADDY
35—SITTING PRETTY

# HER ONLY CHANCE
## Cheryl Anne Porter

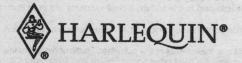

HARLEQUIN®

TORONTO • NEW YORK • LONDON
AMSTERDAM • PARIS • SYDNEY • HAMBURG
STOCKHOLM • ATHENS • TOKYO • MILAN • MADRID
PRAGUE • WARSAW • BUDAPEST • AUCKLAND

To all therapists everywhere.
If you don't have your own book, you should.

ISBN 0-373-25918-2

HER ONLY CHANCE

Copyright © 2001 by Cheryl Anne Porter.

Visit us at www.eHarlequin.com

Printed in U.S.A.

# ____Prologue____

"I ALWAYS KNEW you were crazy."

"Gee, thanks." Jamie Winslow came to a stumbling stop as she jogged with her sister along Bayshore Boulevard. To her left, the waters of Tampa Bay sparkled and winked. Breathing hard, Jamie squinted at Donna through the bright morning sunshine. "Seriously, Donna, I have to go to these therapy sessions. They're required before I can be licensed."

"Yes. I remember those well myself." Jamie's sister, a petite woman with delicate features much like Jamie's own, was bent over at the waist, her hands clasping her knees. Finally, she managed to ask, "But why are you so worried? If you really *were* crazy, they'd already know by now."

"Ha-ha. Very funny." Still, Jamie couldn't help obsessing a little about the tricky ground she and her therapist would cover in that afternoon's session. She was reluctant to mention it to Donna, who always felt compelled to fix her younger sister's problems, even when, like this one, they weren't the least bit fixable. "By the way, Ms. Junior-High Counselor, we in the psychology field no longer refer to people as crazy."

"We should. Most of them are. Except for us, of course." Donna straightened up and groaned. "Every muscle I own hurts right now." With that, she limped off to the nearest concrete bench. Jamie followed her, watching her sister gracelessly flop down on the seat. "So," Donna continued, "it can't be your grades that are worrying you. You've always aced any class you took."

Jamie made a face. "Aced them with a lot of hard work. It was never easy for me like it was for you. But, still, you're right. My grades aren't bad. But apparently I'm a mass of insecurities."

Donna's blue eyes rounded with feigned surprise. "No! Seriously?" She then chuckled sympathetically. "You poor kid. You must be at the part where they tear you down so they can rebuild you."

Jamie nodded, asking desultorily, "How'd you know?"

"Because there's nothing like therapy to unravel a person. Finding out you're susceptible to your own emotions and experiences isn't all it's cracked up to be, is it?"

"No," Jamie griped, crossing her arms. "Now I know how it feels to be a specimen in a biology lab."

Grinning, Donna squinted at the bright sunlight and shaded her eyes with a hand as she stared up at Jamie. "That's the spirit, sis. Seriously, though, try thinking of your time with the shrink as another bit of class work."

"Class work? How?"

"This is where you understand how your patients feel when they come to you and you start doing the same thing to them."

"I see your point. I just wish that was all there was to it." Suddenly overcome with the enormity of her crumbling confidence, Jamie covered her face with her hands and gave in to a moment of pure anxiety.

"Hey, honey, are you all right?"

Jamie lowered her hands and met her sister's concerned gaze. "Do I *look* all right? Donna, what am I going to do? I mean, here you and Mom came all the way from New Orleans to celebrate with me. And I'm not even sure if I'll graduate. I can see it now. Culled from the cap-and-gown herd. Left behind for the predators that prey on the weak and the sick."

"Lord, as bad as all that?" Donna patted the concrete seat next to her. "Come here, Jamie. Sit. Talk to me."

Exhaling her frustration, Jamie sat next to the comforting presence of her sister. "By the way, before we get too deeply into my angst, I want to tell you how good it is to have you and Mom here. Even if it is only for a few days. I miss you guys."

Donna raised an eyebrow. "So move back to New Orleans."

"I can't." Jamie stared down at her running shoes. She could never move back home. Too many bad memories, too much guilt. "I love you all. But my life is here now."

"You keep saying that. And I guess I see your point," Donna admitted. "You've been in Tampa for five years now. I love this city. You've established a nice home for yourself. You have new friends and important professional relationships. And, yes, it will be easier to get a practice going among people who didn't watch you grow up and still think of you as that little brown-haired pigtailed girl with the skinned knees.

But there are times when I wish you'd never applied for the postgraduate opening here."

"It was a blessing, Donna. Trust me."

"A blessing? Then how come you sound ready to hurl yourself into the bay?"

"Oh, please, I'm not suicidal. Far from it." But still, Jamie looked out across the shimmering water and firmed her jaw. *That day* so long ago still haunted her. In a moment of flashback, she relived it. She was thirteen, and her father caught her and sixteen-year-old Kellan Chance together on the bed in Jamie's bedroom. It was her first kiss. It was innocent. A simple exploring of carbonated hormones. And, yes, they had fallen back on the bed. But her father had exploded and thrown Kell bodily out of the house. Then her parents fought, and her father left...for good. God, what a disaster. And it was all her fault. She'd never said that out loud to anyone. It was hard enough to admit it to herself.

Jamie blinked away the bad memory and looked over at her sister. "Trust me, Donna, I would be much worse if I'd stayed in New Orleans."

"What's so bad about New Orleans? You were born there. You have friends there. Mom is there. And I'm there."

Jamie grinned. "You miss me, don't you?"

Donna put her arm around Jamie and pulled her close in a quick hug. "Of course I do, kiddo. I love you. I want you to be happy."

Jamie hugged her back. "I am happy. Well, I was until these required sessions." Jamie's concerns bubbled up inside her again. "Do you realize what will happen if this doesn't go well and I'm not certified to practice?"

"Yes, I do. Ten years of higher education, right along with your career, will circle the drain. But I know you, Jamie. And I know you won't allow that to happen."

Jamie shrugged. "I'll do what I can. But I'm not the only one involved here." *Ouch.* She hadn't meant to reveal that.

"Who are you talking about? Your therapist?"

All she had to say was yes. But Jamie realized she wanted to tell her sister the truth, all of it. She wanted to talk to her. So, adopting a sparkly I-have-a-delicious-secret expression, she said, "No. Not my therapist. There's another 'someone else' I'm talking about."

Donna poked her sister in the arm. "Ohmigod, a man. Talk to me, girlfriend."

Jamie chuckled. It was like they were teenagers again. "Okay. Two words. Kellan. Chance."

Donna stared at Jamie. "Kellan Chance? You're not serious. Come on, you said you haven't even spoken to him in a year."

"I haven't."

"Then what—" Donna stopped and a moment later the invisible I-get-it light went on over her head. She pushed at Jamie's shoulder. "Get *out.* This afternoon's topic on the couch isn't so much Kellan Chance as it is your sex life. Am I right?"

Jamie nodded. "Bingo. My sex life. Or total lack thereof."

"Ah. Not much action since you blew Kell off again, right?"

"I did not blow him off."

"Yes you did. So let me guess." Donna cocked her head, thinking. "I know. You haven't washed that gorgeous, sexy man out of your hair yet, have you?"

"Yes I have." But Jamie's heart knew better. Poof, there he was in her mind's eye. That gorgeous, sexy man, as Donna called him. He lurked inside her...a picture of muscles and a tight T-shirt, of dark and brooding eyes that accused her of walking away from him again. As always, his image sent a delicious shiver over Jamie's skin. Not that all she loved about Kell was sex. But he *was* the type of man that made a woman—any woman—think about the bedroom.

Jamie heard her own guilty sigh in the same instant that Donna did.

"So where'd you go in your head just now?" Donna's grin could only be called lascivious.

Jamie felt her cheeks flame with embarrassment. "Stop that. This is serious."

Donna chuckled and tugged at Jamie's ponytail. "All right, little sister. I'm listening. Talk to me."

"Okay, here's the thing." Jamie took a deep breath for courage and plunged in. "What am I going to do when Dr. Hampton asks me about Kell? I mean, Kell essentially *is* my sex life. There's no way to avoid talking about him." She shook her head. "I am getting such bad vibes for this afternoon's session. It's make-or-break time."

"Yes, it is. So here's what you're going to do." Donna stood up, signaling for Jamie to do the same, and the two of them began walking toward Jamie's car. "While Mom and I are ruining our budgets this afternoon

shopping at Olde Hyde Park, *you* are going to go to
your session and face the truth that you still love Kellan Chance and you always will."

Jamie felt like screaming. There it was, like a big-
banner headline flying across the blue sky for all the
world to see. Her biggest fear just baldly blurted out.
Her denial was instant. "I do not—"

"Oh, you do so. Don't lie to me or to your therapist.
He'll see right through you. Instead, work with the
man to try to figure out why it is that you keep breaking Kellan's heart. And your own."

A second denial rode Jamie's lips, but the words
wouldn't come. Everything Donna said was true. She
couldn't live with the man and she was even worse
without him. And right now, she was without him. Yet
he had the power, without even being aware of it, to
destroy everything she'd worked so hard for.

Jamie sighed in defeat. Loving Kell, or not loving
him, was the last thing she could do anything about.
But it also the one thing she *had* to do something about.

# 1

JAMIE TRIED to remember the last time she'd had a thirty-minute conversation about sex with a man and hadn't at least been turned on first. She couldn't come up with any time before today. Thank God. But now here she was, with her therapist, a slight older man with a gray beard and a notepad, sitting in his private, low-lit office. *Talking about sex.* For thirty minutes!

"I don't have a problem with sex," Jamie assured her therapist for the tenth time. "I like it a lot. Well, at least I did before this conversation. Now I may never want it again." She grinned, but when the therapist didn't even crack a smile, she hurriedly added, "Just kidding. Don't write that down. Okay, so you're saying I have a problem with one member of the opposite sex, right?"

"I don't know, Jamie. You'd have to tell me."

"I did tell you. Sex for me is pronounced Kellan Chance. You'd think the man and I were star-crossed lovers, and I'm compelled to keep reliving the tragedy."

"Tragedy?" Dr. Hampton raised a graying eyebrow. "Is that how you see your relation—" A knock on the door interrupted him. "I'm sorry. Will you excuse me?" He stood up. "Roberta wouldn't knock if it weren't an emergency."

Jamie waved a dismissive hand at him. "Please, go

ahead." Secretly thrilled with this temporary reprieve, she added a smile. "Take your time."

Dr. Hampton nodded and crossed the room, quietly opening the door and leaving the room. Jamie watched him, thinking she needed to develop that soothing technique. She couldn't seem to enter or exit a room without wrenching the door open or banging it closed. If only she could close her aching—and arousing—thoughts of Kellan Chance as easily.

It was true. Where Kellan was concerned, her heart and mind and body simply would not allow her to rest. He was entrenched in her senses. She felt certain she could smell his scent, taste his kiss, feel his touch...even after not seeing him for a year. *No.* Jamie leaned forward, crossing her arms atop her knees and resting her forehead against them. *Do not think about him, Jamie. You'll only lose.*

She raised her head and stared across the soothingly lit and comfortably furnished office where Dr. Hampton plied his psychiatric trade. "I can do this," she said softly to the man's diplomas hanging on the wall behind his huge walnut desk. "I can and I will," she said with more force, already feeling better. "I don't have anything to worry about."

*Except Kellan Chance.*

Slumping, Jamie muttered a mild expletive. *The man is going to drive me crazy.* She then remembered her conversation earlier with Donna about being crazy. Yeah, crazy about Kellan. Worse than that, she knew she still loved him, as Donna had accused. *Not that loving him has done me any good,* Jamie fussed. *Kellan will never change.* She knew it was true. The man, despite all his wonderful qualities, physical and otherwise, was a thrill seeker, a danger junkie. Her exact opposite. He was also, without being aware of it, her worst enemy. Or he would be, if the truth ever got out.

That truth was that Jamie had fallen for Kell—the classic "wrong man"—and hadn't been able to get over him. In fact, she was so hopeless where he was concerned that her academic curiosity had finally taken over and had plunged her into research, which had fueled her doctoral thesis: Women Who Fall For "The Wrong Man": Why Do They Do It?

How could she have known that, in psychology circles, her research and the resulting paper would be hailed as groundbreaking? That was another secret she wasn't able to share with Donna or anyone else—her secret book deal with a major publisher who wanted her to develop her thesis into a nonfiction, self-help guide on relationships. Once she signed the contracts, she'd have a lot of money and even more publicity. But there would be no binding contract until she rewrote her thesis into lay terms, and made it slick and glossy in short chapters chock-full of advice, conclusions, lessons, and, worst of all, answers. *Help.*

The publicity plan scared Jamie the most. The publisher wanted to spring her on the public, present her as the one woman in today's world who had all the answers about relationships. Jamie could read the caption now, headlining her photo on some glossy magazine page: *What does this woman know about relationships that you don't?*

*Not a damn thing.* She still couldn't believe this was happening to her. Who would have guessed that the woman from New York that she'd found herself cornered by at that faculty mixer—all Jamie had known then was the woman was someone important's sister—was also a high-powered literary agent?

Even now, Jamie could remember how, out of sheer desperation for something to talk about, she'd spouted off about the research she'd done, the interviews, her conclusions, et cetera. And then the woman produced a business card, gave it to Jamie and said *Kid, I'm going to make you a star.*

*Whew.* A book like this was all about perception, Liz Clendenen, the agent—*her* agent—had told her. In Jamie, the publisher believed they had the right author, providing she turned out to be an entertaining writer, too. She was young. Attractive. Articulate. Educated. Yep, she had all the credentials, everything they could hope for. All in one package. Except...and only Jamie knew this...she was a fraud. She, too, had fallen for the wrong man. And she still wasn't over him. That made her a victim of her own syndrome. Frankenstein's monsterette. Dr. Jekyll and Ms. Hyde.

*I have to quit bringing up Kellan to Dr. Hampton. He could unwittingly blow the whole book thing, along with my license to practice, if he thinks I have serious unresolved issues here.* Jamie wondered how this could be happening to her. Just when everything fell into place in her life...it all fell apart. She had this unbelievable chance to succeed beyond her wildest expectations, and she'd lost control over her own destiny. Her feelings toward Kellan Chance could torpedo everything.

It had always been this way for her in her life. Every time she tried to do anything positive, something went wrong. No wonder she'd become a thinker, a watcher, and not a doer.

A moment later, she heard the office door behind her slowly opening. Her heart thumping, she quickly brushed her long hair back from her face and tugged at her short skirt. *Just keep your cool here, Jamie. You can do this.* She turned and smiled at Dr. Hampton.

His answering smile bled into a quizzical frown as he sat in his chair and opened his notepad. "You look nervous, Jamie."

"I do? Well, I'm not. Except about getting my license to practice, that is." No license, no certification meant…no book. Only, Dr. Hampton didn't know that, and she couldn't tell him.

He nodded. "Yes. Your license to practice." But he didn't elaborate. He just took up where they'd left off. "Before we were interrupted, you mentioned—" he checked his notepad "—Kellan Chance and tragedy. Tell me about that, Jamie."

"Well, there's no real tragedy. Not like a car accident, or plane wreck. It's just that when Kellan and I get together, it always ends up in heartache, almost as if we were predestined for it. We always come to tragedy, it seems." When the doctor said nothing, Jamie continued, blurting, "Kellan is Gaelic for warrior, you know. And he certainly lives up to his name. He's a Navy SEAL. Did I tell you that?"

Dr. Hampton nodded. "Yes. But there's more to him than that, isn't there?"

"Oh, of course. He's kind, considerate, intelligent. A real Southern gentleman. A well-rounded man." The image that conjured up in her mind…Kell's physical well-roundedness...had Jamie blushing and looking down at her hands in her lap. Why did she always become so wrapped up in Kell physically that she forgot his other attributes?

Dr. Hampton suddenly broke into Jamie's reflective silence. "Those are all good attributes, Jamie. He sounds very nice."

"He is." Her words were a defeated sigh. "He's more than nice. He was my best friend. We did everything together. I miss him—" Jamie watched Dr. Hampton writing furiously on his notepad. What now? What had she said to set him off on yet another blazing round of note-taking? That she missed him? Jamie sat silently, determined not to utter another word until her therapist/professor stopped scribbling her innermost secrets onto what would become nothing more to him than office notes.

The air conditioner suddenly kicked on, sending cooled air throughout the comfortably furnished office. Jamie was sure the walls were slowly closing in on her. Finally, Dr. Hampton stopped writing and looked up at her. Despite herself, she had to admire his expertise. "This works for you, doesn't it? The long silences, all that writing? Just awaiting the patient's thoughts— which they finally and desperately blurt out. It's a good technique."

"Is that how you feel, Jamie? Desperate?"

She stared at Dr. Hampton. He acted as if it was his job to jump on everything that came out of her mouth. Then she remembered...that was his job. It would also be her job someday soon—if she got past these sessions. "Yes, I feel desperate. But desperate to graduate and get my license. That's all."

*Well, now, Jamie, that certainly sounded hostile.* Dr. Hampton probably thought so, too, given the assessing stare he was sending her way. Swallowing, Jamie glanced at the wall clock behind him. The obnoxiously slow-moving big hand showed she still had fifteen minutes left in her hour. *Great.* Jamie smiled hopefully, helplessly, at her therapist and wisely said no more.

Dr. Hampton carefully placed his notepad on the small table next to him. He brushed something off his trousers, crossed his thin legs and met her gaze. *Bad news* was written all over his face. "You come back to your license almost as much as you do to Mr. Chance. I don't suppose, though, that I blame you. Only I'm afraid, Jamie, that your license isn't going to be forthcoming, at least not yet."

His words were like an arrow to the heart of her future. Jamie put a shaking hand to her temple. "Would you please explain 'not forthcoming'?"

"I'm afraid it means I'll be, well, holding up your license."

Jamie's heart raced, leaving her weak-kneed. *Her license.* Her agent had called her just three days ago asking her when she'd have it. Liz had said Jamie needed to mail a copy to Highline Publishing and to her the day she got it. Only then would they draw up contracts that meant a signed deal. Jamie could hear herself assuring Liz she'd have it within a week or so. Or so? Suddenly "or so" appeared to be sometime in the next Ice Age. "Oh, God. Oh, please, Dr. Hampton, you can't deny me my license. You can't."

Dr. Hampton's gaze roved over her face. "I'm not going to deny you your license, Jamie. Well, not for any longer than I have to. I just think there's something here that needs fine-tuning, let's say."

*Fine-tuning? That's it?* Jamie leaned forward and stared at her former mentor, now tormentor. "That sounds hopeful. Considering I've studied under you for years, you'd have seen if I had any serious emotional problems by now. We're just talking about temporary, right?"

"Correct. And I don't feel you have serious emotional problems, Jamie. However, I am seeing something, in the course of these sessions, that I feel you need to address before going into practice for yourself."

*But I'm not going into practice,* she wanted to yell. *I'm going to be rich and be on TV. I'll have books and make public appearances and—*

Dr. Hampton continued "—while I don't think you have a long-term problem, I just don't see how, at this point, I can recommend you for licensing in marriage and family counseling."

Still a bit breathless with the enormity of the man's words, Jamie concentrated on breathing—and cooperating. "Okay. So we can't do that now. What do I have to do? More classes? Labs? Some more interning?"

Dr. Hampton held out a steadying hand to her. "No, none of that. You've been exemplary in your courses. It's not that at all."

"Then what? It's me, isn't it? You're just being nice and I am so totally messed up, aren't I?"

Dr. Hampton chuckled. "No, calm down. You're going way overboard with this."

Yes she was, and she couldn't stop it. "Am I at least going to graduate tomorrow night? I have family here for the ceremony. What am I going to tell them?"

Dr. Hampton gripped Jamie's hand and looked her in the eye. "Listen to me. You don't have to tell them anything. You *will* graduate tomorrow night, and your degree *will* be conferred upon you. It will be my honor to present it to you, Jamie."

Grateful tears filled her eyes. Jamie slipped her hand out of his and reached across a small end table to the box of tissues. She plucked one out, wiped her eyes, then tossed it in a waste backet. "Well, thank God—and you—for that much, at least. My mother and sister are here from New Orleans to see me graduate."

Dr. Hampton smiled. "Excellent. I'm sure you're enjoying their visit. And I'll look forward to meeting them." Then his expression sobered, signaling a change in subject. "About your license, Jamie. Try not to be discouraged. Or too hard on yourself. I think you can work through this just fine. However, your graduate committee and I believe that before we can sign off on your state application you need to work a bit on finding closure."

Jamie nodded, taking a moment to come to terms with what he was telling her. She also tried to think how she could get through this without Liz finding out. She had no choice but to cooperate. And to admit that this had really shaken her. Was there no area in her life where she could get things right the first time out? "All right. What do I have to do?"

"As I said, seek closure. With Kellan Chance."

Jamie's stomach tightened. As Donna had reminded her, she'd walked away from Kell—for the second time in her life—only a year ago. And now, her entire professional life rested on achieving closure with this man, a consummate warrior in her white-collar world? A teensy little fly in her great big jar of ointment? Dread washed over Jamie. Resting an elbow atop her knee, she leaned forward, rubbing at her forehead. "Great. Kellan Chance. The story of my life. I thought you meant undergo more sessions, talk about my feelings for him, something like that."

"I do. We'll continue those as well."

"Dr. Hampton, perhaps I should explain. Kellan and I have quite the history. We go way back. Since before high school. Then, eight years ago, when I was twenty-one, I left him at the altar. Full church, white dress, all the trimmings. He was not amused at being humiliated in front of the whole town."

"I suppose not. So you're saying you don't believe Mr. Chance has feelings for you?"

"Oh, he has a lot of feelings for me. All of them centering around murder."

Dr. Hampton eyed her skeptically. "Are you certain? Because you said earlier in this session that you'd been involved with him after the, um, failed wedding."

Guilt had Jamie darting her gaze around the room. "Yes. Two years ago we got together again. We lasted about a year."

"I see. And how did it end that last time?"

"Badly. I walked away. Again."

"Ah. Why is that?"

Jamie was getting tired of this being all about her. "Look, you need to understand the Chance family. It isn't just a name with them. It's their motto. The whole family takes chances in some way. Kell has two brothers—Brandon and T.J. Brandon is older than Kell. He used to be a Nightstalker pilot. Now that he is out of the military, he's still taking risks, running his own security company. And T.J., the youngest, is into extreme sports. *Very extreme.* Even their parents are gamblers—*real* gamblers. That's how they earn their living. So anywhere it's legal, they're there. When the boys were young and the Chances needed to go 'earn a living,' they'd have Aunt Tillie—who deals cards on a riverboat—sit with them."

"Good heavens."

"That's milder than most people put it." She stopped and looked Dr. Hampton in the eye. "And that's the crux of the problem. I just don't think Kell could change, even if he wanted to. And I don't think he does. Taking risks is in his genes. He gambles with his health, his life, his body. Everything but his heart. He—"

"Jamie, what would you do if he *did* change?"

Her body's response to that question startled Jamie. Fear had jetted over her. Fear, not relief. Warily, she eyed her therapist. "What do you mean?"

"If he quit taking risks. If he settled down, got a stable job. Would you marry him?"

"Wow. I can't imagine Kell like that." She laughed. "No, I guess he wouldn't be himself, so I wouldn't love him as much as I do. So I couldn't marry him."

Dr. Hampton just stared at her.

Jamie sobered. "Oh, God, I am *so* messed up. How could I get this far without knowing myself?"

Dr. Hampton relented, smiling. "I see this all the time at this stage, Jamie. We're so busy learning and examining everyone but ourselves that we forget we're human, too. I'm simply saying there's something here worth exploring. Some unresolved feelings between the two of you. Do you agree?"

Jamie's shoulders slumped with defeat. "Yes." What choice did she have?

"Don't look so glum, Jamie. You've made real progress in the past few weeks."

"I suppose. I'm almost *not* against marriage anymore."

Startled, Dr. Hampton sat forward in his chair. "That's an odd conviction, Jamie, for someone who's training to be a marriage and family counselor."

Jamie started backpeddling before she lost more ground. "I'll be a good counselor, Dr. Hampton. You know that. Just because something isn't right for me doesn't make it wrong for other people. I can separate the two."

"Well, the only way we'll know that for sure is for you to achieve a satisfactory resolution with Mr. Chance. In fact, I think your success in private practice depends on it."

This was a disaster. Jamie exhaled slowly. She'd give anything if she could tell him the truth, that she wouldn't be going into private practice. Then it struck her. It didn't matter if she went into private practice or not. She'd still need the same skills, the same compassion, when she wrote her book because she'd still have patients, hopefully millions of them. Her readers.

Dr. Hampton was right. Facing Kell again would only make her a better therapist, a better author—a better person. Dammit. She brushed her hair back from her face. "So. Kellan Chance."

Dr. Hampton nodded, seemingly a bit mollified. "Afraid so. But I don't think it's as dire as you believe."

"Oh, it's dire. I am the last person on earth Lieutenant-Commander Kellan Chance wants to see."

"You've said as much. But isn't he stationed here in Tampa at MacDill Air Force Base?" He flipped back through his notes. "Yes. Here it is—Special Operations Command, right?"

"Right," Jamie grumbled. She knew how close Kellan was to her...geographically.

"Good. Because if you take care of things with Commander Chance promptly—then we might not have to delay your licensing for long."

"Seriously?" Jamie perked up. "How long?" Maybe she could stall Highline Publishing. Maybe she could tell them her license was being processed. She could plead logjammed paperwork, delays at the post office, things like that.

"Well, how long depends on you. But I'm thinking maybe thirty days."

Relief coursed through Jamie. Thirty days were so doable.

"I believe that since Mr. Chance lives here, all you need is opportunity."

Jamie shook her head. "And more courage than I've ever had." She could just see herself knocking on Kell's door...after having told him, a year ago, that it was over forever between them. She could still see his stony expression that hid the hurt in his dark eyes. Guilt pushed aside her short-lived relief. She couldn't play with Kell's heart for her own gain. She had to be sincere in whatever she said or did. Or she'd never respect herself again. "So, all I have to do is get him to talk to me, just work out our issues? I mean, I don't actually have to commit to anything with him, do I?"

"Oh no, no. We're not in the business of forcing love. I wouldn't counsel that. But, Jamie—*is* this something you can do? Do you feel safe, comfortable, in his presence?"

"Safe?" She thought of Kellan's hawkish stare, his muscled body...the way his hands, his mouth, felt on her. She sighed. "Safe and comfortable are two things no one feels around Kell. He's so intense. But in this context, yes, I'll be fine. Despite his training and his occupation, he's a very gentle man. Out at the base, the Special Ops guys are called the Quiet Professionals."

"I see. That's interesting—and good to hear. Because all I'm asking you to do is examine your own motives and feelings and then talk to him."

"Talk to him," she repeated. "This whole thing sounds as if I'm seeking forgiveness."

Dr. Hampton's expression softened. "You may be. But you won't know until you talk to him."

Just the thought of seeing Kell again had her stomach fluttering...with anticipation or dread, she couldn't say. Heaving out a sigh, she met her professor's waiting gaze. "So. I guess I have my marching orders." She looked at the clock. Mercifully, her hour was up. Jamie stood and retrieved her purse. Dr. Hampton stood, too. "This isn't going to be easy," she remarked.

"I know. If it were easy, you wouldn't have a problem." With that, Dr. Hampton walked her to the door. "Try not to worry right now, Jamie. Get through graduation and enjoy your family's visit. After they leave, we'll talk again and go from there, okay?"

Jamie opened the office door and then turned to shake his hand. "Thank you...I guess."

Dr. Hampton chuckled. "Jamie, you're one of the finest doctoral candidates I've ever worked with. You're infinitely qualified academically, and you'll be fine. Trust me, this Kellan Chance thing is merely a hump you need to get over. One day you'll look back on this and thank me—only sincerely."

While pleased by his compliments—her flagging confidence really needed to hear them—Jamie just smiled. But she couldn't help wondering if, once she walked back into Kellan Chance's life, *he* would want to thank Dr. Hampton. Yeah, right. With a low-level air strike, maybe. Or a bouquet of bayonets.

# 2

MEANWHILE, and not too far away, on the secretive air force base situated on a spit of land that jutted out into Tampa Bay, Kellan Chance was learning his fate. And he was not a happy SEAL.

"I just don't see any help for it, Lieutenant Commander," General Halter was saying. "Your medical condition requires me to assign you thirty days R and R while we make a further review of the incident. While you're on the mend, you're free to come and go as you please. But I'd like you to stay in Tampa and make yourself available to the investigators."

"Yes, sir. Of course, sir." No one had to tell Kell what his commanding officer meant by thirty days of rest and relaxation. He had, in essence, just been relieved of his command, wounded or not. Dressed in his battle fatigues in front of General Halter's desk in the Special Operations Command headquarters building on MacDill Air Force Base, Kell knew he'd messed up. He'd been in charge of a mission in Eastern Europe that had gone sour.

It was the worst possible outcome. They'd been detected, had a face-to-face with the opposition, and in the ensuing fight, some of his men had suffered injuries. In fact, Jeff Camden, his second-in-command and Kell's best friend, was still in the hospital in Frankfurt,

Germany. Guilt ate at Kell. Still, he refused to blame the bad intelligence he'd received regarding their target. He had no one but him to blame. That was the way it worked. He knew the risks and had always accepted them. With rank came responsibility. He'd danced to the music, and now it was time to pay the piper. Hopefully, the price would not be his career. That loss of honor would be unthinkable.

"At ease, Commander. This isn't an inquisition."

"Yes, sir." No less tense, Kell did as ordered. He stood straight, his hands clasped behind his back, his gaze riveted to a point on the opposite wall.

"Look, Kell, why don't you sit down and let's talk, man to man?"

Kell blinked at the general's familiar use of his name. He cut his gaze over to the tall, lanky man, who suddenly appeared to look a little haggard. "Yes, sir. After you, sir."

The general nodded and sat down, gesturing to the upholstered leather chair on the other side of the desk.

With measured precision and a few sharp moves worthy of a military parade...as if to show the general that the sutured and bandaged cut on his thigh didn't bother him...Kell sat, holding his Special Ops beret in his hand while he awaited the general's next words. He tried to convince himself that his heart wasn't about to thump out of his chest.

The general sat forward, resting his elbows atop his desk and tenting his fingers together. "All right, here's the thing. How old are you?"

Startled, Kell almost dropped his precise military bearing. "I'm thirty-two, sir."

"Thirty-two. And you're a lieutenant commander. I've always believed that only in our profession and in professional athletics is thirty-two getting up there in age. Most of our field officers are still in their twenties."

Kell knew instantly where this was going. A desk job. His chest tightened around his heart, which felt as if it were expanding. "Begging the general's pardon, sir, but I'm as fit as any man in my—"

"Yes, you are, even despite your injury. And you're a fine commander. Your men are extremely loyal to you, and your superiors sing your praises, me among them. You're also a highly decorated officer with more successful missions under your belt than anyone else. No one doubts your dedication, son."

*Until this last mission.* It was unspoken between them. As the general talked, Kell's jaw got tighter and tighter.

"It's time for a change, Kell. I know how you feel about a desk job. But you have to admit this isn't any ordinary office. You know what SOCOM is—a mixed-branch military nerve center where the strategy is done for the four services, where the missions originate. And it's a tremendous responsibility. I feel we need someone like you in-house. No one knows Special Ops like you. And, of course, there's a promotion in this."

Kell sat rigid. The only thing worse would be to get assigned to the Pentagon—it was considered a graveyard for commanders. However, the one-foot-in-the-grave assignment was the desk job. Which he'd just been handed. A dead end. The last of the line. Kicked off the team for a lack of performance. Total loss of respect, of self-esteem. And there wasn't one damn thing he could do about it, except say, "Thank you, sir. I'm honored, sir."

"Like hell you are, Commander. I wasn't when I got these stars—" he pointed to the insignia of his rank on his shoulders "—and this corner office. I thought my military life was over, that I was washed up. I couldn't have been more wrong. And neither can you. This isn't punishment, Kell. But it will seem like it when you're sitting here safely, knowing you're putting young men out in the field in jeopardy. You're going to fret like you're their daddy. And you'll find you're extremely careful of every detail so none of them gets hurt. That's what I want from you. In one way, having you here is a way of making sure that what happened to you and your men will never happen again."

Kell met his commanding officer's steel-gray eyes. The general was referring to the intelligence officer who'd been relieved of command after Kell's latest mission had failed. But Kell couldn't help thinking that the general also meant that if Kell was sitting here at a desk, he couldn't lead any other men into a trap. He swallowed, knowing the general was awaiting some comment from him. He stood up, coming again to attention. General Halter followed suit. Kell met the older man's gaze. "Thank you, sir. Will that be all, sir?"

The general looked Kell up and down, narrowing his eyes assessingly. "You're a fine man and a fine officer, Commander Chance. It's just time for a change, for a move up the chain of command. It will be an honor to have you in the building and to work with you directly."

Like the general had said—it sure as hell didn't feel like an honor. Still, Kell put his beret back on, carefully adjusting it to the perfect angle. Then he saluted the general. "Thank you, sir. I look forward to the opportunity to serve you and my country in my new capacity."

The general nodded and returned Kell's salute.

Guilt ate at Kell. He'd gone too far one time too many. He'd asked too much from his men, and they'd almost paid the price with their lives—and all at his command. Maybe the general was right. Maybe he was getting too old for this. Maybe it was time to quit gambling, something his parents had never learned. Maybe it was time for a desk, time for change. No more risks.

Like hell it was. A bit of the fire in Kell's belly went out. Who was he kidding? He didn't believe any of that. He was Kellan Chance. A warrior. It was too bad his mother and father had just left after coming to see about him. He could have asked them what the Gaelic term for desk jockey was. Thank God they'd returned to New Orleans before he'd been put out to pasture. That wasn't something he wanted them to know right off. But he'd better get used to the idea, he told himself. Because apparently he was going to have to live it.

He was also going to have to find a way to avoid losing face with his risk-taking brothers. Or himself.

THREE DAYS and as many doctoral-degree celebrations later, Jamie sat with Donna in the sun-splashed Tampa International Airport. True to Winslow form, the three of them—Jamie, her sister and their mother—had arrived chronically early for the flight that would take Jamie's family back to New Orleans. So, with time to kill, their mother had wandered into a glass-fronted bookstore in search of the latest thriller to read during the flight.

That left Jamie and Donna to chat as they camped out with the carry-on luggage at one of the upscale coffee bars in the terminal. But even with all the traffic around them, all heads turned their way when Donna squealed, "You have *got* to be kidding—"

"Shh." Jamie immediately leaned across the table. "Mom and half of Tampa will hear you."

Donna's blue eyes danced with delicious intrigue as she, too, leaned forward, speaking in a lowered voice. "Mom's over there in that bookstore. She can't hear us."

"Ha. The woman can hear through walls. We're talking about Mom here, Donna." Jamie sipped the last of her coffee.

"Like heck we are. We're talking about Kellan Chance. I was right, wasn't I? You're going to have to confront him." Triumphant, Donna sat back. "Damn. I'm good."

Jamie wondered what her sister would say once she could finally tell her about the book deal. "Yes, you are. But I knew it would all be about Kell, if you'll remember."

"Yes, you knew." Donna turned serious. "But I'm worried about you, little sister. You walked away from that man *and* a church full of people on your wedding day eight years ago. And then you broke up with him again last year. And now these psycho professors of yours want you to see him again?" Donna sipped her coffee and eyed Jamie over the cup's rim. "Have they lost their collective minds, playing Cupid like this? Kell is not going to be amused."

"They're not playing Cupid. They say I need closure. Can't you just hear me telling someone as practical-minded as Kellan Chance that we need closure? He's going to think I'm crazy."

"Well, add my name to that list," Donna said. "I've thought you were nuts ever since you ditched him right out of college."

Jamie let out a guilty breath. "Will you quit saying I ditched him? I didn't ditch him. I had...issues."

"Issues? Such as...?"

"It's not obvious? The way he plays with life and limb, Donna. I mean, come on, he's thirty-two now. When do these Chance boys get over it?"

As if suddenly too warm, Donna fanned herself with her hand and sent her sister an arch expression. "They're hardly boys, honey. Whew. Kell and his brothers are men to the nth degree. Wow." Then she popped forward in her seat. "Wait a minute. You knew that Kell hadn't changed a couple of years ago when y'all got back together. Shoot, we expected you two to finally get married then. But you took off on him again. So, what's really going on here, Jamie? There's something else, isn't there?"

Jamie exhaled and toyed with her now empty paper cup. There *was* something going on. She just wished she knew what it was. It wasn't a commitment thing. She'd committed to many things...although none of them had been men.

"Sweetie? Out loud."

Jamie blinked and stared at her sister. "Oh. Sorry." Suddenly she wished she and Donna lived a little closer. There was no one better to confide in. Donna was a counselor herself, a committed wife to Wayne and a wonderful mother to Jamie's niece and nephew, Cindy and Bret. In other words, she was stable. But Donna was also someone who would be totally on Jamie's side, someone who had the same parents, the same experiences, and who could tell her how to get past this closure/commitment hang-up of hers.

Feeling a rush of warmth for her sister, Jamie leaned forward, fully prepared to spill everything that was going on with her—including the book deal. Until she glanced over her sister's shoulder. Then Jamie sat up stiffly, her mouth open, her eyes wide.

Donna pivoted in her seat and a starkly silent moment passed. Then, Donna, still looking over her shoulder, intoned, "Oh...my...God." She jerked back around to face Jamie. "Is that who I think it is with Mother?"

Jamie nodded and finally remembered to breathe. Kellan Chance was walking their way. He was almost upon them...with her mother in tow. And that wasn't all. Latched on to his arm was a stunningly beautiful woman who smiled warmly up at him.

KELL GLANCED DOWN at Melanie, who clung tiredly to his arm. Her flight from Germany, not to mention the long hours she'd spent at her husband's bedside, had to have been exhausting, but still she smiled up at him. Kell winked at her and then met Jamie's gaze as they approached the table where she sat with her sister. Jamie's expression reeked of uncertainty. For his part, though, Kell could hardly look at her without wanting her. His breath caught. His chest ached. Dammit, he wasn't the least bit over her. Still, staunchly military in his bearing, despite his civilian clothes, and revealing nothing of his inner turmoil, Kell proceeded with his greetings. "Donna, Jamie," he said, managing a sincere smile. "It's good to see you." His gaze came to rest on Jamie. "You look great."

Some naked emotion flared in her eyes but was quickly gone, leaving Kell to wonder if he'd really seen it. But if Jamie had nothing to say, Donna wasn't stuck for words. She got up immediately and came around the table toward him, her slender arms held out. "Kellan Chance, you great big hunk of good-looking man, come here and give me a hug. Excuse me." That last was meant for Melanie, whom she neatly sidestepped as she wrapped her arms around his neck and hugged him hard.

Held that way, Kell could only submit with a grin. When Donna finally released him, he stepped back, glanced again at Jamie, who hadn't moved except to tightly cross her arms and legs. All Kell wanted to do was sit down and memorize very nuance of her. He wanted, needed, to feel the heat from her body, smell the scent of her skin, hear her laugh, listen to her talk. But he couldn't. He turned to Melanie. "Donna, Jamie, I'd like you to meet Melanie Camden. Melanie, I've known Donna and Jamie since I was a kid back in New Orleans."

"That he has," Mrs. Winslow chirped, her bright-eyed gaze and forced smile betraying her underlying nervousness. "Isn't Melanie just the prettiest thing, girls?"

"Lovely," Donna confirmed, arching a worried look at Jamie.

Fighting a grin, Kell silently applauded Jamie's mother's attempt at diplomacy. No doubt, she expected the same fireworks from her daughter that he and, obviously, Donna did. "Why, before I recognized Kellan, I couldn't help thinking, 'What a lovely couple.' And well, I guess they still are. Don't you think so, Jamie? Honey?"

Along with everyone else, Kell looked expectantly at Jamie. Finally, she got up and came around the table. "Yes, Mother, they're very lovely." Then, offering her hand to Melanie...as if a firing squad forced her to do so...she said, "Hi. I'm Jamie Winslow."

"It's nice to meet you, Jamie. It's good to meet all of you." Melanie retrieved her hand and brushed it through her sleek brunette hair. "Kell always speaks of New Orleans and his family and friends there. And looking at y'all, I can see it's no wonder. All that rich mahogony hair and those blue yes. How striking. Louisiana must be missing three of its sharpest beauties."

In Kell's opinion, this just could not get any better. The three women, like everyone else from three to ninety who met Melanie Camden, softened and sighed, succumbing to her Atlanta-debutante charm that even out-Southerned theirs. You couldn't hate the doe-eyed Melanie if you tried. Kell knew that Jeff, her husband and a Tom Cruise look-alike, counted him as the only man he could trust with his wife—but only in broad daylight and in a crowded airport. She was that breathtaking—and that upsetting to Jamie. Kell didn't know if he felt good or bad about that.

"Are y'all just getting in? Or are you leaving?" Melanie asked, apparently feeling a need to fill the gap in the polite conversation that none of them were making.

Jamie, Kell noticed, studiously avoided looking at him as she answered. "My mother and sister were here for my graduation. They're leaving today."

"Oh, I'm so sorry. Why, I bet you hate to see them go," Melanie sympathized. "But how nice for you...your graduation, I mean. What a happy time in any family. May I ask what degree you obtained?"

"She got her doctorate in clinical psychology," Mrs. Winslow chimed in, as if anxious for an opportunity to praise her daughter. "We're so proud of her. She's a doctor now."

Kell, tired of being ignored, reached out and took her hand in his, holding it tightly...even as that familiar fire traveled up his arm. "Congratulations, Dr. Winslow." He looked her right in the eyes. "I know how much getting your degree means to you. In fact, I recall it was more important to you to get a degree in mental health than it was to practice it yourself."

He'd left her no choice. Jamie bristled. That was what he wanted from her...an honest response. "I don't practice mental health? How about you? Jumped out of any perfectly fine airplanes lately? While they're in the air, I mean."

In light of last week's secret and disastrous events, Kell bristled right back. "As a matter of fact, I have. Just recently I jumped out of an airplane that was only barely adequate."

"Oh, really, Captain Marvel? No parachute, either, I suppose?" She jerked her hand, trying to get it out of his grip. But Kellan wouldn't let go, he couldn't let go. Jamie's face reddened. He knew that sign—her Irish was up. And he knew what would follow. An escalation in the cold war.

"You're so full of yourself, Kellan Chance, you probably just floated to the ground on your own ego."

"All right now, you two, that's enough." The sharp intervening warning came from Jamie's mother. "Don't you start up in front of Melanie here. Behave." Then she turned to Melanie. "Think nothing of them, honey. They've known each other practically since the cradle and just fuss all the time."

To Kell, Melanie looked shell-shocked. Jamie finally managed to pull her hand from Kell's and touched Melanie's arm. "I apologize, Melanie, for my rudeness. But if you'll excuse us, I have to get Mother and Donna to their terminal. Their plane leaves in—"

"An hour. We have plenty of time...Dr. Winslow," Donna said, cutting Jamie off and emphasizing *doctor*...as if reminding her to act her profession, if not her age.

Kell's anger left him. He'd provoked Jamie and this scene. It was up to him to end it. He gripped Melanie's elbow. "It was nice to see all of you. But I'm sure Melanie's luggage is downstairs at baggage claim by now. If you'll excuse *us*."

Everyone—except Jamie, Kell noticed—called out goodbyes and nice-to-have-met-yous. As he walked away with Melanie, Kell thought he could still feel Jamie's hand in his, as well as her gaze burning into his back. He wanted nothing more than to turn around, stalk back to her, grab her by the arms and kiss the hell out of her...for starters.

After a few more steps, Melanie broke the silence between them. "That's her, isn't it? She's your lost love—the one whose name you'd never tell me."

Suddenly defensive, Kell shrugged. "She might be."

Melanie tsked. "Might be, nothing. She is, and you know it. I swear, Kellan Chance, if you don't tell that woman you still love her, you are just going to pop."

Kell's jaw tightened. "Then I guess I'll have to pop."

"Oh, you men. You are so stubborn."

Kell glanced down at Melanie's beauty-queen face. Guilt shot through him. Her worry over her wounded husband, the exhaustion on her face, her long flight...all of that was his fault. He'd caused it, as much as did the hazards of belonging to Special Ops—or being married to it. Kell suffered the fleeting yet troubling realization that this woman's life, lived essentially without her husband at home but always worrying about him, would have been Jamie's, if the two of them had made it work that last time. This is what he would have been subjecting her to. How selfish was that? Kell blinked away his unsettling epiphany by grinning down at Melanie. "What about you women? You go around breaking our hearts all the time."

Melanie demurred with a classic uptilted look at him through her long eyelashes. "Only as necessary. And always for a good reason."

Kell laughed. Even more than Melanie's beauty, he appreciated her for her warmth and wit...two of the same qualities he'd always admired in Jamie. "I'm in over my head with you, aren't I?"

"I expect so."

"You do know that Jamie thought you and I are together, don't you?"

"Well, we are together. But I know in what sense you mean."

"And you were content to let her think it, weren't you?"

Melanie raised her chin, à la Scarlet O'Hara. "As were you. But from what I just saw in that woman's eyes when she looked at you, this isn't the last you've seen of her. Now, what do you think of that?"

Kell couldn't deny the leap his heart took at such an idea. But out loud he quipped, "Frankly, my dear, I think I don't give a damn."

THE NEXT DAY, Jamie flopped impatiently around her high-rise apartment, dressed only in shorts and a T-shirt. Nothing felt right. Even the brilliant Florida sunshine, sparkling off the blue water of the bay outside her balcony's sliding-glass doors, couldn't cheer her.

That's what she got for setting up the next two weeks as her downtime before beginning the arduous task of trying to make a glitzy bestseller out of her doctoral thesis. She'd known this time would be all she'd have to herself for a while and had looked forward to the freedom. But now the days seemed ominous, as if each passing second was stretched taut and yet frighteningly short. All because of Kell.

Standing now at the closed glass doors, her arms

crossed, Jamie watched a jogger slowly progressing along the same stretch of sidewalk that she and Donna had run. And decided she'd never felt more alone. She tried to tell herself that what she was experiencing was simply the normal letdown following the excitement of graduation. After all, her academic life, for the most part, was now over. That was good, she supposed.

And then there was Mom and Donna. She'd really enjoyed their visit, just the three of them, girlfriending it all around Tampa. There'd been so much to show them. But now they were gone. Back home. A wistful feeling overtook Jamie. She'd hated not being able to tell them about the book deal. It had taken every bit of restraint she possessed to keep it a secret. But a signed deal was a signed deal. She was to tell no one. And she hadn't.

It was funny. She wanted this book contract mostly because of the good she could do with the money that came with it. And yet she couldn't tell those it would affect. Jamie hated that her mother, who'd already suffered one heart attack, was still working and paying off a mortgage. Her mother had even managed to help Jamie through college, just as she had Donna. Now it was time to pay her mom back, to give her a carefree life, full of fun and travel, whatever she wanted. It was only fair. And her mother was still a relatively young woman of fifty-eight. She could find someone else to make her happy. Jamie smiled, knowing nothing would make *her* happier than giving back even a little of what her mother had given her.

So her silence now about the book deal had been bittersweet, even more so as she'd watched her family leave. Their leaving always left a void and yesterday had been no exception. Again, she saw herself standing at the plate-glass window at the airport, watching the big jet take off, already missing them.

She'd been sad...and seeing Kellan had made her feel so much worse. Jamie felt so hollow, so fragile. It had upset her to realize that she'd wanted nothing more, as he walked away with that woman, than to humiliate herself and chase after him, crying out his name, begging him to stop. What a desperate, romantic scene that would have been. Like the foggy airport scene at the end of *Casablanca*. *Of all the homecomings and leave-takings that go on day in and day out at airports all around the world, you had to walk into this one.* Or something like that.

Still, she couldn't get yesterday's scene out of her mind. There she'd sat, unaware of his nearness, enjoying the moment with her sister. Then, out of the blue, Kell and that gorgeous Melanie Something had walked right up to her and Donna. What were the chances that her mother would run into them in a complex the size of Tampa International Airport? *Stupid fate.*

*Poor Mom.* Before she'd gotten onto the airplane, she'd said she was sorry. She simply hadn't known what to do once she'd realized it was Kell she'd bumped into. She'd been stuck and had to bring him over and she hoped she hadn't upset Jamie. Jamie recalled now downplaying the moment, telling her mother that was silly, she was over him and had been for a long time.

*Yeah, right. I'm over him.* Tears threatened in Jamie's eyes. She blinked and sniffed, telling herself she could not do this. Not for a license. Not for a publisher. She just couldn't contact Kell now that she knew about Melanie. *Another woman. Talk about closure.* Jamie knew she should be happy for him. He'd gotten over her, that was easy to see. But it hurt. Turning away from the glass doors, Jamie told herself she needed to shake herself out of this mood before she did something dire...like eat all the ice cream she had stashed in the freezer. She perked up... *Hey, ice cream. That sounds good—*

The phone rang. Blessedly.

Relieved for her waistline, Jamie ran for the cordless set, flitting around her furniture and hoping it was either Becca or Jan or Carrie—or all three of her friends, women who understood the terrible possibility of death by chocolate. They could all go out to lunch. Or for a ride to the beach. Or shop. No, wait, this was Monday. They'd all be at work. So who could be on the line? She grabbed the phone on the third ring. "Hello?"

"Jamie? It's Kell."

Jamie froze, staring at her reflection in the ornately framed beveled mirror over the sofa. The woman staring back at her looked shocked. *Because that woman is,* Jamie told herself. Her heart was pounding and she felt hot and weak and giddy.

In the earpiece she heard Kell saying, "Jamie? Are you there? Do I have the right number? Is this 2-5-8—"

"Yes. It's me—" she swallowed, having trouble saying his name "—Kell. I'm just...I'm here. Hi."

"Hi. You okay?" His voice sounded low and seductive. It frittered on Jamie's nerve endings.

Despite their public fuss yesterday, she strove for

light and cheerful. "Sure. I'm fine. Couldn't be better. How about you? You okay? How's Melanie?"

After a second or two, Kell said, "She's fine. All safe at home after visiting her husband."

"Her *husband*?" Jamie was shocked. What he did and who he saw were really none of her business. But considering she had the home field advantage with him—meaning, she'd known him since he was a kid—she could be judgmental. "Kellan Chance, you're seeing a married woman? What would your mother say?"

"Nothing, because there's nothing to say. Melanie, just like her husband, Jeff, is a good friend of mine." Kell chuckled. "Not that I owe you an explanation, but I was just seeing her home after an overseas flight."

A bit embarrassed, Jamie tried to keep the moment. "Oh, a world traveler, huh? Must be fun."

"Not this trip." Kell's voice was dark. "Jeff was...injured and is in the military hospital in Frankfurt, Germany. Melanie had been over there with him. So when she flew back home, I offered to pick her up. It's the least I could do."

They were friends. *Just friends.* Jamie's heart soared. Kellan didn't have someone else, and he wasn't over her. She knew this because he'd just gone to great lengths to explain things to her. "That was nice of you to help out a friend," she finally said. "So how's her husband? Is he going to be okay?"

Kell didn't say anything at first. After a few moments, he said, "Jeff will be fine. Melanie wouldn't have come back otherwise." She heard him let out a loud breath. "Listen, Jamie, I really called to apologize to you for what a jerk I was at the airport yesterday."

She couldn't believe her ears. "What's this? An apology from *the* Kellan Chance?"

He chuckled. "Knock it off. I'm trying to be nice here."

"Wow. Now I'm worried. I must be dying and no one's told me. I mean, an apology *and* an attempt to be nice—all in the same conversation?"

"People change, you know. You probably wouldn't recognize a lot of things about me now."

Jamie tensed, again assailed with the same fear that had gripped her when Dr. Hampton had asked her what she'd do if Kell ever changed. Suddenly claustrophobic, she searched for something innocuous to say. "So, were you and your friend Jeff on some mission when he was injured?"

"You know I can't say if I was there or even if it was a mission."

Which meant it had been and Kell had been there. Still, something in his voice, a sadness or a hardness, she didn't know which, made Jamie ask, "Kellan, are you all right?"

"Yeah. I'm fine."

"You don't sound fine." Now that she thought about it, yesterday he'd looked thinner. His handsome face had been all taut angular lines. And he'd walked stiffly, too, maybe a bit slower. Then, because he was so somber, so different, and because she was worried about him, Jamie reverted to familiar ground. "So, are you still Mr. Important out at MacDill?"

That earned her another chuckle...a sound she knew well and loved, one that had her stroking the mouthpiece in her hand, as if by doing so she could feel Kell's strong jaw or his clean-shaven cheek. "Ironically," he said, "I'm even more so now, it turns out. And how about you, Dr. Winslow? I'm really proud of you—not that you could tell yesterday by my behavior at the airport."

"Forget that, Kell. We were both pretty immature. The shock of seeing each other, I guess. I'm over it."

"Well, good. But I'm still sorry. So, are you going into private practice?"

Jamie exhaled in frustration. When would she ever be able to tell anyone the truth? "No. Not exactly. Why? Are you in need of a therapist?"

"Surprisingly, yes. It's been suggested."

Jamie laughed. "I bet it has." But she already knew that the men of the Special Forces units regularly undergo psychological testing and evaluation because of the nature of their jobs.

"So, Jamie, how come there's no new man in your life?"

Well, that touched a very old and deep wound between them. But his voice hadn't sounded anything but conversationally friendly...maybe. "Now, how do you know there isn't? I could just be going by my maiden name, you know."

"That's true."

He didn't believe her in the least. Mainly, she decided, because he knew her too well. After all, he was the man she'd twice left standing alone. There it was— the old commitment thing. Jamie smiled wistfully. "I can't pull anything over on you, can I?"

"No. Afraid not."

After that, the conversation seemed to drag. Jamie

couldn't think of a thing to say. And all Kellan did was breathe...and perhaps wait for her to say something. She wondered why he'd called, where this was going. "Are you married, Kellan?" she suddenly blurted.

"Oh, hell no. You broke me of wanting that. Ever."

Well, if she thought the conversation had lagged before...

"Look, Jamie," Kellan suddenly said, "you want to get a drink or something right now? Maybe ride to the beach, if you don't have plans?"

He was asking her out? "No, I don't."

"You don't what—have plans or want to?"

He was so direct. And giving her the opening she needed to speed up the closure Dr. Hampton so obnoxiously insisted on. Jamie moistened her lips. She couldn't think how to respond. It suddenly seemed cheap to use him like this. Especially when he was down and a little vulnerable. But wasn't that the perfect mood for him to be in for her to achieve her goal? *Well, that sounds perfectly noble, Dr. Jamie Lynn Winslow.*

"Hello? Jamie?"

Jamie started, as if only then realizing she held a cordless phone to her ear. "Oh, I'm sorry, Kell. You just surprised me, that's all."

"I didn't mean to. But what do you say?"

He sounded as if he really needed to talk to her. This was so scary and so unlike Kellan. Jamie's chest constricted. Why was she so good at this with patients but terrible at it in her own life? "No, Kell. I...can't go with you. I'd like to. But I can't."

"Can't or won't?" His voice betrayed nothing.

Helplessness ate at her. She didn't want to turn him

down. She wanted to go, but she feared it was for the wrong reason. For her reason. And not his. If he was really down, then he deserved honesty and sincerity. Not her self-serving motivations. "I just can't. I'm really sorry, Kellan."

His silence told her he clearly hadn't expected that response. Just as she was about to change her mind, he said, "All right. If you can't, you can't. Sorry I bothered you, Jamie. I shouldn't have called. I guess I just let the past get in my way there for a minute. It was nice seeing you yesterday. I was just hoping—well, never mind. It won't happen again. Goodbye."

Jamie started to protest...but the line went dead.

# 3

THE HOLLOW SOUND of a dial tone assaulted Jamie's ear. Hating herself, she hit the off button, and tossed the cordless set onto her overstuffed sofa. She followed it, plopping down on the poofy cushions. "Jamie Lynn, why didn't you go?" she asked herself. "Because I—"

The phone rang again.

Startled, her pulse racing, Jamie searched the cushions for the receiver. And came up with it on the fourth ring. "Hello? Kellan? I'm sorry. I—"

"Jamie? This is Dr. Hampton. Are you all right? You sound breathless."

"Dr. Hampton? Oh, hi. No, I'm fine." Acute disappointment ate at her. It wasn't Kellan. Of course it wasn't Kellan. Why would he subject himself to further rejection? "Did I forget a session?"

"No, no. We need to schedule one, if you'll remember. I told you I'd call you the first of the week. Remember? And this is Monday, Jamie."

"I know what day of the week it is, Dr. Hampton. I am firmly oriented as to day and time."

"Of course you are, Jamie."

That's when it hit her. He was right—this *was* Monday. Why wasn't Kellan at the base? How could he be free to ride to the beach on a Monday? That didn't make sense. He never took time off. Jamie frowned. Something *was* wrong with Kellan.

"Jamie?"

"Oh, sorry, Dr. Hampton. I'm right here. When did you want to see me?"

"That depends on you. Have you had an opportunity to speak with Mr. Chance?"

"Sort of." When Dr. Hampton didn't say anything— it was like being back in his office—Jamie rushed to explain. "I mean I had a chance—no pun intended—encounter with him yesterday at the airport. And he just called me a few moments ago."

"Oh. That explains why you thought I was Kellan."

Caught red-handed. "Yes, sorry. But the conversation between us didn't go well. As usual."

"I'm sorry to hear that. I guess we couldn't expect it to be smooth sailing right out of the chute."

Jamie frowned. A mixed metaphor from Dr. Hampton? It really was Monday. "No. I guess not."

"May I ask why it didn't go well?"

"Sure. You're the guy with the license." She had to wonder why she was always on the defensive with Dr. Hampton.

"You're being defensive, Jamie."

She exhaled sharply. The man missed nothing. "I know. I can't seem to be any other way with you."

"Just relax and let me help. So, I guess we'd better set up an appointment. How is Thursday afternoon at three, shall we say?"

As if she had any plans. "Fine."

"Good. That gives you another three days to talk to Mr. Chance. In the meantime, give some thought to a specific plan. Be proactive in this. Set some goals so you'll know if you're making progress. I think that will help you." Dr. Hampton paused. When he spoke again, his voice held a different tone, that of a friend...or a father. "I wouldn't ask you to do this, Jamie, if it weren't important. I might be your therapist, but I also like you very much. You're a wonderful young woman with a bright future. I have been proud to call you my student...and now, hopefully, my colleague and friend."

Tears clogged her throat. She'd never seen this side of Dr. Hampton before. "Thank you," she managed to sniff out.

"You're welcome." Then, he turned professional again. "Well, then. Does meeting with Mr. Chance remain something you're comfortable doing?"

*No.* "Yes. But you know, he seems sort of down about something, Dr. Hampton. I don't want to use him for my purposes, if he's really vulnerable right now."

"That's very admirable, Jamie. But you wouldn't be using him if you were sincerely listening to him and being his friend. In fact, why don't you strive for that, for just being his friend? You might be able to help him. After all, you are a trained professional, as the joke goes, so you *can* try this at home. Come up with a non-threatening situation for your first meeting. Maybe a ride to the beach?"

"Well, that's already been discussed. Apparently, I should be listening. Anyway, thank you for your advice. I'll be Kell's friend, and I'll see you Thursday at three."

"I look forward to it."

"Me, too. Bye, Dr. Hampton." Jamie hit the off button again and just sat there, the phone in her lap, staring into space.

She'd just blown Kell off and now she had to reestablish contact with him. *Fine. But on my terms, not his.* That was why she'd refused him when he'd called, she told herself. She hadn't been comfortable with the scenario. His car. His money paying for their drinks—he would have insisted on that. Kellan calling the shots. The balance of power would have been all wrong. She needed it to be on her side when she talked to him about closure. Her closure. Not his.

Jamie frowned. *Now, that sounded terribly selfish.* It brought back Kell's remark yesterday about her thinking everything was about her, and that bothered her. Maybe the problem was she spent too much time considering every motive behind every act that every person ever made. Well, hadn't she just spent the last ten years training to do exactly that? So why should she beat herself up about being true to her profession? *Alleged profession, if I don't find closure.* So there it was. Maybe she was trying too hard. Maybe she just needed to lighten up and concentrate on other people. Wasn't that what her profession was all about, anyway? Helping others?

But she knew that she had to be okay with herself first before she could be of any help to others. She couldn't be like the dentist with bad teeth. Or the beautician with awful hair. She had to be the therapist with her head—teeth, hair and all—on straight. And that meant...she had to deal with Kellan Chance. Just his name made her shiver with wanting. It was so masculine, so strong. Gaelic for warrior. Jamie put a hand to her forehead and closed her eyes. "Oh, man. What have I got myself into?"

She jumped up off the sofa and stood there, her hands on her waist. Kellan Chance. He made her body do the craziest things. She wrapped her arms around her waist, hugging herself. Why could she never forget him? In the past year, she'd dated a lot of other men. Greg. Hank. John. But they hadn't been able to measure up. Her memories of Kell had ruined every relationship. She'd hardly got past the initial attraction stage with the other guys before she lost interest. And they'd been nice men, too. Sharp. Professional. Funny.

Everything Kell was...but less than him somehow.

Jamie's eyes widened with insight. Apparently she'd tried, in each new relationship, to find Kell all over again. Only she'd looked for men who either didn't feel they needed to risk their very lives every day or didn't have professions that required it. Like Kell's did. Yet, in comparison, they'd bored her to tears, with their talk of advertising, stock brokerage, yacht-building. *Yawn.*

"Great. I am one sick puppy. I hate the fact that Kell risks his life and yet I don't want anybody who won't take chances."

Disgusted with herself, Jamie padded over barefoot to the sliding-glass doors at her narrow balcony that overlooked the briny blue waters of the bay. She opened the door and stepped out onto the railed enclosure. Surely, over four billion tourists a year couldn't be wrong. This place was supposed to be inspiring. She closed the door behind her and plopped down on a patio chair. Maybe just enjoying the atmosphere would help.

After a few moments, Jamie realized that she did feel a little better. The sky was blue. A slight breeze stirred her hair. *Like a day at the beach.* There it was again. Jamie frowned. On a Monday? She couldn't get past that. What was he doing off work? He'd sounded as if he could come get her at the moment.

That was something Kell would do, too. He wasn't one to take no for an answer. She smiled, and found herself half wishing he'd come anyway. Then Jamie realized what she'd been thinking. She was hoping that Kell would force the issue, rather than have her take responsibility. Jamie leaned forward, resting her crossed arms along the wrought-iron railing. *What do I want? What will happen if I'm around Kell again?* But she knew. She'd lose control. She always did. Just one look, one touch...and she ended up in Kell's bed—naked. She didn't know how it happened. It just did. Every time. *Hi, Jamie. It's Kell.* Bam...she was naked. Emotionally, if not literally.

And that was the part that scared her the most. The emotional exposure. She sighed. *That damn Kellan Chance.* Maybe this time she needed to take a different approach...like being a friend. Well, they'd been friends first. Couldn't they do that again? Tell each other their hopes and dreams. Talk about the future. Things like that. That's how it had been when they'd been younger, before their raging hormones had taken over. Could they recapture some of that innocence?

Jamie knew that the past was behind them. But they

could still talk about what was going on with them now. She sure had a few problems she wouldn't mind discussing. Maybe Kell did, too. But would he accept her as just his friend? Didn't he have Melanie for that? Maybe. But Melanie didn't know him like Jamie did. Melanie hadn't seen him through all his bruises and broken bones. She hadn't known him when he'd been a skinny boy with a dirty face who tried so hard to live up to his family name. Jamie smiled, suddenly filled again with love for the boy that Kell had been. Couldn't she still be that boy's friend?

Jamie straightened up...excited, energized. That was it. Dr. Hampton was right. She and Kell would go back to being friends. She would have to initiate it, though, since she'd just turned him down. So, what was the plan? Well, the first thing she needed to do, she decided, was to tell him they needed to talk. Then she would make him understand what was at stake here—the book deal. Then she'd have to apologize for dumping him twice. And if she was lucky, her *friend*, would go with her to tell Dr. Hampton "mission accomplished." One simple conversation. That should be all it took to get her licensing.

Jamie put a hand to her forehead. *Oh, Kell, I don't think I can do it.* She wondered how she could pretend to feel only friendship for the one man whose touch made her bones melt. Okay, so she wasn't over Kell. But that wasn't what this was about. You could love someone but not have him in your life because he wasn't good for you. Wasn't that the crux of her research, anyway? What she needed to do was accept that Kell was the one—the wrong one—and move on.

*Yeah, right. The man can burn me up with one look.* Yesterday in the airport, his dark eyes had bored into hers and when he'd said she looked good, she hadn't been able to breathe. Jamie blinked, rousing herself. She didn't have time for this. If she wanted her license she was going to take the biggest chance of all.

THE DOORBELL RANG. Still not quite awake, and cursing softly at the interruption in what for him was a rare afternoon nap, Kell went downstairs and opened the door. There stood Jamie Winslow. Even dressed in nothing more exotic than khaki shorts and a white sleeveless blouse, she looked like all of his favorite fantasies come to life. His heart skipped a beat. "Jamie."

"Hi. We have to have sex."

Kell stared at her. It took him a second to filter what she'd said. He leaned against the doorjamb, crossed his arms over his bare chest and forced his gaze to remain on her pretty girl-next-door face. "Tell me you're not going door to door with that line."

She grinned brightly. "Oh, but I am. And you're my first stop."

"Well, lucky me." Kell snatched her right off his sunbaked front porch and into his town house. Toeing the door closed behind her, he took her into his arms, crushing her against him. With her face lifted to his and her mouth opened—no doubt, to protest—Kell gave her no chance to speak. At this moment, he wanted nothing between them. Especially not words.

Heatedly, with a kiss every bit as hot as his need for her had been since seeing her yesterday, Kell claimed her mouth. He couldn't seem to help himself. Nor did he want to. His thumping heart had nearly leaped out of his chest when he'd opened the door to see her standing there. Even now he couldn't stop himself from devouring her. He needed her more than he needed his next breath. But though she responded, he felt her tense against him, pushing him away.

Kell pulled back, looking into her face.

"My purse," she said breathlessly. "It's in the way." With that, she carelessly tossed her bag down and again melted against him, kissing him feverishly, her soft breasts pressing provocatively against him, her palms running up his bare chest and sliding across his shoulders.

Kell felt her possessively wrap her arms around his neck, just as she'd wrapped her them around him in his late-night dreams. Dreams that always ended with him in a sweat and his sheets twisted around his legs. Dreams that left him, aching for the one sweet body denied him, the one sweet woman he could never seem to hold on to. But now, here she was. In his arms. In his town house. Exactly where he wanted her.

A moment later, Jamie broke off their kiss. "Oh, Kell. Wait. I can't catch my breath."

Kell gripped her arms, holding her out from him as he looked down into her face, one he'd loved all his life. "I can tell." His adrenaline surged. "And you're not the only one, Jamie. Wow."

She extricated herself from his grip and stepped back, taking a deep breath and fanning her face with her hand. "Wow is right. We still do that well, don't we?"

"We always did. It was the rest of the stuff that kept us at each other's throats."

She sobered. "That's so true. And that's why I'm here. I really wish we—" She bit down on her bottom lip and frowned.

Kell called himself a stupid jerk for attacking her. *What the hell is wrong with me?* But he knew. Around Jamie Winslow, he lost control. Every time. And lately, it seemed as if he was losing control in every aspect of his life, including his career. Maybe he *was* getting too old. Kell ran a hand through his short-cropped hair. "I'm sorry, Jamie. I shouldn't have grabbed you like that. I had no right."

They were still standing in Kell's tiny foyer. Jamie shrugged. "Hey, I'm not upset. It wasn't like I didn't want you to kiss me. I mean, what were you supposed to think, given my opening line?"

Kell grinned. "You're right. And, by the way, I'm on board with the two of us having sex. If you say we have to, then we just have to. I'll consider it my patriotic duty."

Jamie's expression relaxed. "Very funny."

"Yeah, well, since looks aren't everything, I've been working on my social skills. That kiss was my new greeting. What'd you think of it?"

Jamie's eyebrows raised. "I think if you greet everyone that way, then I'll bet you have trouble getting a pizza delivered. Or not...if your delivery person is female."

Kell chuckled, but couldn't look away from her blue eyes. It struck him that here they were, talking innocently while their eyes were sending heated messages and making love. He tore his gaze from her face, only to find himself staring at her hardened nipples, which were not the least bit hampered by being bound in a lacy bra and a thin white blouse. "So, Jamie, it's nice to see your, uh, sense of humor is still intact."

"Thanks." Jamie pointedly crossed her arms over her chest. Kell met her gaze but couldn't quite kill the grin on his face. Jamie retaliated by lowering her gaze to his...below-the-waist area. "Well, look at this. This is certainly progress for us. We've been together for five minutes and you're still wearing your pants."

Kell looked down at his navy-blue sweatpants, and was glad to find that his desire wasn't quite as evident as it had been a moment ago. "Keeping my pants on is part of that social-skills thing I was telling you about. I've instituted a new policy of not answering the door in the buff."

Jamie's eyebrows raised. "That *is* a good policy."

"The pizza delivery guy thinks so. So do the police."

She laughed. It was what Kell had been waiting for—neutral territory. "So, you want to start over?" he asked.

Her grin faded. "Start over how?"

Kell held up a hand. "Easy. I mean like having a normal conversation. Like, 'Hi. How're you doing?' A conversation that had nothing to do with sex. Regrettably."

Jamie seemed surprised. "That's exactly what I came over here for, believe it or not." She grinned and crossed her arms. "So, Kell, how are you doing? How's the family?"

Kell shrugged. "I'm good. The folks are good. They were just here."

"They were?" Disappointment clouded her features. "I would have loved to see them. A social call, I hope?"

She knew him too well. "No. Not completely. I was in the same, uh, accident that Jeff Camden was."

Jamie's gaze swept worriedly over him. "Oh, God, Kell, are you all right?"

Her concern for him heartened him. "It was no big deal. Just another stupid stunt of mine."

"I don't think I've ever heard you call anything you did 'stupid stunts.'"

"Well, I told you, I'm a changed man. Hey, did you know that Brandon and Serena got married? They're on their honeymoon right now."

Jamie smacked at his arm. "I know. Donna told me. I couldn't believe it. I never knew they were more than just friends. And what's T.J. up to nowadays?"

"Hell, he's as bad as me. He's off on some extreme adventure somewhere. Aunt Tillie told me, but I forget the details."

Jamie shook her head. "I don't know who's worse. You Chance men or your Aunt Tillie." Then she roused herself and became all business. "Look, about this visit...well, I need to talk to you and come to some kind of closure."

Kell crossed his arms over his chest. "Closure on what?"

"Us."

"I thought we already had that."

"Not as much as you'd think." Looking hesitant, Jamie glanced around. "You mind if we sit down?"

"Oh, hell, I'm sorry." They were still standing in the foyer. He'd gotten so caught up in her being here, and in kissing her, that he'd forgotten his manners. "Sure. Come in." He waved a hand toward his overstuffed sofa. "Have a seat."

Jamie grabbed her purse and preceded him. Kell unabashedly watched her walk toward the sofa. Long-legged. Slender. Curvy. Just the way she moved, like a torch song come to life. Kell had to make a conscious effort to be in the moment. It was damn hard because he just couldn't believe she was here, or how her presence rattled him. Some things never change, he lamented. "Make yourself comfortable. I'll just go put on a shirt. Then I'll fix us a drink or something."

"That sounds great." Jamie sank onto the cushions, put her purse to one side of her and then rubbed her temples.

"I'll be right back," Kell said, but for some reason his feet wouldn't move. It seemed his gaze was riveted to hers—and she wasn't looking away. A storm cloud of emotion billowed between them. Kell inhaled against the tightness in his chest and managed to get a single word out. "Right."

It was enough to break the sensual spell...for the moment. Turning away, he stalked over to the stairs and, despite his sutured thigh, sprinted up them to the second floor. In his bedroom, he spied his discarded T-shirt on the bed. Snatching up the black shirt, he pulled it over his head and tugged it down his torso.

In only moments he was back downstairs, sitting next to Jamie. "So, what's this sudden need for closure?"

Jamie looked down at her lap a moment and then at him. Concern edged her blue eyes.

Overwhelmed by a sudden fear for her, Kell swallowed hard. "Are you okay, Jamie? Is something wrong? You're not sick, are you?"

She frowned. "No, not physically. I'm fine. It's just that...well, after your call today, I guess I just got a little worried about you."

Kell stared at her, not knowing what to think. His emotions, always off-kilter around her, flared...and came down on the side of perturbed. He sat forward. "I see," he finally said, feeling more than stupid now for having kissed her. "So this is a sympathy call?"

She frowned. "Do you need sympathy, Kell?"

He sat back. "No, I don't. Just what the hell did I say that made you think I might?"

"Now you're getting defensive."

"I probably am. Because this visit of yours doesn't make sense. I call you, you blow me off, then you show up here saying you need sex and closure. Now you're here out of sympathy for me. What the hell gives?"

"I'm trying to explain. But apparently I'm not doing a good job of it. It's just that it struck me as odd that you would call on a weekday, and want to take a ride to the beach. That's not like you. I got worried after I thought about it, so I came over."

Kell nodded. "Yeah, you did. But with a line about us having to have sex."

"I was just...trying to be funny. Get over it."

"All right. I'm over it. What next?"

Jamie exhaled sharply. "I swear, you can be so— I just want to know if you're okay. Is that so hard?"

In the grip of rising anger, made all the worse given how her proximity affected him, how her nearness made him want to touch her, Kell sprang to his feet. "Hell, yeah, it's hard, Jamie. I told you a year ago that if you left, it was over between you and me. And you left. Now, here you are again. Damn, that's not fair."

Kell watched as Jamie squeezed her eyes shut. Her chin quivered. He wanted nothing more than to take her in his arms and hold her. But he didn't. He couldn't, even though her slenderness seemed painfully fragile somehow.

A moment later, she opened her eyes and sought his gaze. "Kell, I really didn't come here today to fight with you. Or to jerk you around. Or even to try to start something up between us again. But...well, do you suppose I could have a soda or something, please?"

Kell frowned at her switch in subject. "A soda it is." It took an act of will, but he walked away from her, going to the kitchen and opening the refrigerator. He got out two cold sodas and twisted the tops open. But keeping his hands busy didn't stop his thoughts from churning. Weren't his career problems enough to bear? Did *she* have to show up now, too? Jeez, why had she been the first person he called, when she was the last person he needed to see? He walked back into the living room and handed her the drink. "Here you go."

"Thanks." She took it and held it, not drinking, just watching him.

Feeling under the gun, Kell again sat next to her. He took a long swig of his soda. Then turning to her, he ran his gaze over her face again, taking time to note her fine-boned features and their contours, every one of which he knew intimately. His gaze met hers and held. Electricity sparked between them. She hadn't said a word as she'd watched him. Watched him what? Reveal that all he wanted to do was hold her and have her tell him it was all going to be okay—when he knew it wasn't? Not with her and not with his career. Pulling back from his thoughts, and how they made his gut knot, Kell indicated her untouched drink. "Thought you were thirsty."

"I am." She took a drink and then surprised him by slipping her free hand into his. "Kell, seriously, are you all right?"

Her tone, as much as her sympathetic gesture, unnerved him. Kell realized he was squeezing her hand, returning her warm pressure. He pulled away. "I'm fine."

Feeling a need for some distance from her body heat, he set his soda on an end table and got up, crossing his small living room to stare out the sliding-glass doors. The tropical greenery of the courtyard failed to hold his attention. Peering over his shoulder at Jamie—his first love and, dammit, probably his only love—he asked, "So why'd you turn me down earlier?"

She shrugged. "That's complicated. I still had some thinking to do. And some things to answer for myself. I just wasn't ready to see you right then."

"But an hour later, you are. So I'm guessing you got your answers." When she nodded, he turned to face her, allowing his gaze to travel over her, from her thick dark hair to her red-painted toenails peeking out of her sandals. He had but one thought. If he didn't maintain his distance, he'd end up on his knees in front of her with his arms wrapped around her legs, begging her to—to what? Love him? "So what were these questions you needed answers for, Jamie? I assume they had something to do with me or you wouldn't be here."

He watched as she carefully put her soda down on a table next to her. "Kell, I was worried about you. That part is true. But I'm also having a little trouble getting my license to practice psychology."

Kell choked. "I can't say I saw that one coming. What has that got to do with me?"

She smiled wryly. "More than you could ever imagine. Apparently, I can't move ahead until I burn all my bridges behind me. Close the gate on my past. Our past as a couple, actually."

Kell frowned. "Again, I thought we already did that. But I'm listening."

"Okay. Basically, we need to talk. I thought, before I came here, that all we'd need to do was have one productive conversation and wrap this up. But...being with you again, Kell..." She took a deep breath. "I think I was just fooling myself. I realize now I'm not willing to...I can't just tell you..." She lapsed into silence and looked away.

Kell waited, his heart hammering with a yearning to hear her say something provocative. Something like *I still love you.* Yeah, right. Like he needed or wanted to hear that. How many times in his life was he going to set himself up to hear goodbye from this woman? How many times was he going to hear how they could never be together because of his job and her fears for him? Hell, nothing had changed. And he didn't need this aggravation.

Jamie chose that moment to speak again. "All right, Kell. What I need from you is time and cooperation."

Relieved—and a little disappointed—Kell thought of his month of enforced rest and relaxation. "Well, as blind stupid coincidence would have it, I'm on leave for the next thirty days. Will that be enough time?"

Jamie's expression brightened. "Yeah. Sure. That's great. Thanks." Then her expression fell. "Wait. You're on leave for a month? Kell, what exactly happened to you that you'd need a month off? Tell me."

Wounded pride on two scores—his failed mission and his failed relationship with her—made it hard for Kell to keep his frustration under control. "I didn't need or want a month off, Jamie. I was told to take it. But, look, let's get something straight here. You asked for my help. I said yes. But that's as far as it goes. You have no right to ask me how I'm doing. I'm not one of your patients. You walked out a year ago, and we said that was the end. Now here you are again, wanting more and I don't know that I have anything to give. This *is* a bad time for me. But it's a private, personal matter, one that I don't feel like sharing with you or anyone else."

Silence greeted his outburst. "Wow," Jamie finally said, her eyes rounded. "I guess you told me."

"I guess I did."

She exhaled, her gaze seeming to look right through to his hurting heart. "Does this have anything to do with your friend Jeff?"

Kell's jaw tightened. "You don't give up, do you? I said don't go there."

Jamie sighed, a sound laden with resignation.

"You're right. Your problems are just that...yours. And mine are mine. So, I think I'll just leave, Kell." Defeat laced her words. "And you're right about something else, too—I was wrong to come here. Although, in one way, I now have what I came for. Thanks."

She stood up, retrieving her purse and pulling out car keys. Her fingers worked agitatedly around her key ring. "Thanks for your time and the soda," she said, her innocuously polite words belying the heavy drama of the moment.

Kell ached, just looking at her. He swallowed around the lump in his throat. All he had to do was...nothing. And she'd leave. But somewhere, in some deep and dark place inside him, he knew that this time...if he let her walk away...he'd ever see her again. Ever.

Kell swallowed again. The lump in his throat made it feel as if he were being choked. But still he got the words out. Three words that could make all the difference in his life. Whether for good or for bad, though, he had no way of knowing right then. "Please don't go."

# 4

JAMIE DIDN'T GO. But it wasn't for closure. This time was for beginnings...for opening her heart and her arms and her body to Kell in ways she never had before. They were like two wounded animals seeking comfort in each other. In Kell's bed, locked in his embrace, Jamie knew this time was unlike all the other times they'd had together. Before, their coming together had been out of healthy lust mixed with genuine love and affection. But never before had they come together like this, out of a sheer physical need born of a hunger in their souls.

It was the most amazing thing for Jamie, being here in Kell's bed, in his arms. Kell needed her. He truly needed her. And she needed him. She hadn't even known it until she'd stood in front of him again today. She hadn't realized how much she had missed him...missed his touch, his voice, even his intensity. But most especially, she'd missed the way he was holding her now, the way they fit together, the way her body opened for him, took him in, wrapped itself around him. Jamie had forgotten the luxury of being with someone this familiar. Their lovemaking was like a choreographed dance, a torrid work of art all itself. Kell knew just what to do...and when. And so did she.

The sweet blissful torture built inside Jamie with

each thrust of Kell's hips against hers. She clung to him, raking her nails across his back, breathing in short gasps and calling out his name. Even though he labored hard against her, he murmured sweet words of love into her ear that drove her crazy. Then suddenly it was there, the moment she'd hungered for, the moment her body burst in its joy at having Kell inside her. He tensed, holding himself rigid over her, and Jamie took up the motion, moving her hips in a timeless rhythm that increased her pleasure to the point of madness. A hoarse cry escaped Kell. He called out her name, thrust once more against her, and then...he collapsed atop her. Jamie welcomed his weight. Welcomed it and reveled in this most intimate of embraces.

They spent the afternoon, either in a pleasant, sated buzz...or on the thunderous roll of athletic sex. They alternately made love, dozed contentedly, and even did some talking. "Thank God you're still on the pill," Kell said with a grin.

"I know. It wasn't as if you had boxes of condoms in the drawer."

"I've been out of the country. Didn't need any where I was going."

With her head nestled in the crook of Kell's shoulder, Jamie spoke softly. "You could have said you didn't need any because I wasn't around."

"All right. I didn't need any because you weren't around and I've been celibate for a year."

"Liar."

He chuckled. "I'm not lying. There's only you for me."

"Liar."

"It's true, but I give up. I can't win here."

"No, you can't. But are you going to tell me how you got that huge gash on your thigh?"

"No. Sorry, I can't."

Jamie knew what that meant—he'd been injured on a mission—but she let it go for now. "It's obviously a fresh wound...but may I say it didn't seem to bother you just now, Romeo."

He chuckled. "My whole damn leg could have fallen off and I wouldn't have cared."

Jamie didn't comment. Instead, she fought the old but very real fear for his safety that was a constant sore spot between her and this man. Her heart thumped in mortal fear for his life. But she was determined to respond differently. Her former behavior had gotten her into this mess. "I'm glad you weren't...hurt any worse, Kell."

He shifted position, forcing her to look into his dark eyes. "That's it? That's all you have to say?" His disbelieving gaze searched her face. "Before, you would have pitched a fit and stormed out because of something like this. You would have told me how we could never have a life together because I'd be off somewhere all the time and you'd be left behind to worry."

"God, I must have sounded like a shrew. But you're not the only one who's grown and changed. Although I still don't see *how* you've changed." She leered at him, then smoothed her hand down his belly to his crotch and took him in her hand. He gasped and tensed. "Or *where*, either," she purred, grinning. "Everything looks and *feels* the same to me."

Kell gently pulled her hand away, kissing her palm.

"Leave me alone," he teased. "You're wearing me out. Remember, I'm thirty-two now and recovering from a wound. One that came damn close to keeping me from getting any older."

His words made Jamie freeze inside. He'd always thrived on close calls. But this last one he seemed to have left him shaken. For some reason, thinking of him as a fragile and vulnerable human being scared her worse than when she'd thought of him as a fearless and therefore invincible warrior. She recalled all the times he'd told her, in his life-or-death profession, any hesitation could spell the end.

Weighed down with her fear, Jamie again rested her head against his shoulder. "As close as that, huh?"

"As close as that." His voice was grim.

He could have been killed. Her worst nightmare. Jamie squeezed her eyes closed and tried to inhale around the tightness in her chest.

After that, there was silence. Where did they go from here? Jamie mused. Was it time to decide to renew their relationship...or to call it quits again? Jamie's answer came to her quickly. It wasn't the one she wanted, but it was the right one.

*I can't do this again to Kell.* The thought, as well as the conviction behind it, was sudden and blinding. Forget the book. Forget the money, the fame, all of it. There was no way she going to play psychology with Kell in the name of some elusive closure. To her, Kell's terrible vulnerability came first. This was not the time to play with his head, which was how she now saw her intentions.

Not for the first time, Jamie told herself she didn't

deserve the book deal if she couldn't even abide by her own research-based conclusions. Because clearly Kell was the wrong man for her. All wrong. And yet, here she was, in his bed. Again. She loved him. There was no sense denying that. But she couldn't live with the terror of his humanity and she didn't intend to. He could continue to choose to put his life in danger. He could continue to live his life apart from those who loved him the most. But it was *her* choice whether or not she would throw her heart into the ring of fire that defined the parameters of Kell's life.

Kell might be feeling his age and starting to pay heed to the caution that came with experience and wisdom. But Jamie knew he wouldn't resign. He'd continue until something put an end to it. That was how he lived his life. And she couldn't bear to sit around and wait for that to happen.

She needed to get out of his life, just as she'd done before. But for a different reason this time. Kell wasn't just a stumbling block to her wealth and fame. He was the man she loved and he deserved better than that...starting now. Jamie sat up, naked and sated with Kell's loving. She shoved her hair back from her face. "Kell, I haven't told you the whole truth. And doing so now might cost me a million dollars."

Frowning, Kell jackknifed to a sitting position next to her, leaving his lower half covered by the sheet...barely. "Whoa. Hold on. What are you talking about? Don't tell me you've become a spy and you're here to seduce secrets out of me."

Jamie made a tsking sound. "Hardly."

But as Kell smoothed his strong fingers up her bare

arm, she almost wished she were. "So what's this about a million dollars?"

His touch did unfair things to her. He was stroking her neck and jaw with his knuckles...in a slow sensuous slide that made her shiver. His raised eyebrows said he'd noted her reaction. In a sweat to get her words out before the two of them lapsed again into lovemaking, Jamie clutched his hand and held it in her lap. That was another mistake because her body was bared to his touch and his hand was close to the heat of her very center. Grinning, he tried to wriggle his fingers loose, but she held tight. "No, Kell. Wait. I'm serious."

"Then you're going to have to let me move my hand. And you'll have to put on some clothes. Because anything you say while you're naked, I'm bound to agree with, only to regret it later."

"What was that—a presex Miranda statement? 'You have the right to be clothed before we talk.' But you're right." She released his hand, firmly placing it in his own lap, and pulled the bedspread around herself as she would a towel following a shower. "All right, is this covered enough for you to think properly?"

"Jamie, you could be covered by a mountain of dirty laundry and I still wouldn't be able to think around you. But go ahead...take advantage of me."

Jamie winced. "I wish you hadn't said that. Because that's exactly how I feel."

Kell's expression sobered. "Oh, really? How?"

Perspiration beaded on her forehead. Kell looked dangerous—defensively dangerous and detached. It was probably this very look that made him so effective in his profession. But Jamie knew she was the chink in his armor. The one who could ultimately destroy him. She hadn't really appreciated that until this moment. Dr. Hampton had been right. Where she was concerned, Kell kept letting her right back in, no questions asked. He did risk his heart—and she didn't. All this time, she'd thought it was the other way around.

"You're awfully quiet, Jamie." Kell's voice was soft, questioning. "What's going on? Is it that closure thing?"

Close to tears—saying goodbye to Kell was the one constant in her life and it hurt like crazy every time. She nodded. "Yes, it is. But it occurs to me that the closure isn't mine. It's yours."

"Meaning?"

"I need to get out of your life. Right now." She tossed the bedspread aside and started to scoot across the bed. He snaked his hand out, capturing her arm and her attention. Naked, vulnerable, Jamie stared into his eyes, seeing anger and determination in his strong jaw.

"Not so fast. I want an explanation. I *deserve* one, Jamie."

Jamie sighed. "You're right. But can we get dressed first?"

His expression mirrored defeat. "Yeah. Maybe we should." He released her and got up from the bed.

Jamie did likewise, hating how they silently, politely, gathered up their clothes and dressed, taking great care not to touch. It was nothing like the way they'd shed their clothes. Garments had gone flying. And touching and kissing had ruled the moments leaving them breathless and urgent. But not now. Now their actions were slow and deliberate, as they put on the armor of civilization. It was like being kicked out of the Garden of Eden all over again. Just get your fig leaf and get out.

All too soon, they were back in the living room. There was nothing left to do but for Jamie to talk. "Okay. First of all, I have a chance at getting a book deal that will set me—and mom—up for life."

Kell lifted his eyebrows. "Damn. A book deal? What'd you write?"

"I haven't written anything yet." Knowing that it was their history together that had sparked her thesis, Jamie strove to sound clinical. "When I do get it written this summer, it will be nonfiction. Sort of a self-help or a how-to book. It's based on my doctoral thesis."

"Sounds interesting." He quirked his mouth. "So, what was your thesis about?"

"Uh...relationships."

He nodded, considering her...in the same manner he probably would an enemy whose neck he was contemplating breaking. Gone was the tender sensual man she'd spent most of the afternoon with. In his place was a warrior. "What kind of relationships?"

She had to struggle not to look guilty. "Those in which a woman repeatedly falls for the wrong man."

"You mean like us, don't you? So what was this afternoon, Jamie? Am I your guinea pig to see if your advice works?"

Jamie's face heated up. "I don't see it that way. And quit being a defensive male."

"What's that? Chapter One...'The Defensive Male'?"

Exasperation ate at Jamie. "This isn't a book about male bashing. I don't feel that way, and I wouldn't write something like that."

"Right. So this research had nothing to do with us? And by the way, congratulations."

Jamie looked down, fiddling absently with her fingers. "Thanks. And, no, it doesn't have anything to do with us." She looked at him, hating the steeliness in his eyes. She knew the signs. He was shutting himself off from her. "Okay, yes. It does."

"I thought so. So I'm the wrong guy for you. That's interesting."

Jamie exhaled. "It's more like I'm the wrong woman for you."

"Don't you think that should be my decision?"

Jamie's heartbeat slowed. This conversation was taking on the undertones of an interrogation. "Oh, come on, Kell. *Do* you think I'm the right woman for you? I mean seriously."

"You have to ask? Didn't we just spend the entire afternoon upstairs in my bed making each other happy?"

"But that was just sex."

"Just sex? Thanks. *Now* I'm beginning to feel used."

"I didn't mean it like that."

"I think you did." He put up a hand to stop her protests. "Forget it. It's okay. We told each other a year ago it was over. And I guess it is. Hell, what's a little sex between friends, right? I guess I'm the one to blame here. After all, I did call you first."

"I would have called you if you hadn't called me."

"You don't have to say that."

"But it's true. I had to talk to you."

Kell jumped up from the sofa and paced away a few steps. He turned to her, crossing his arms over his chest. "So," he said angrily. "Give me the straight psychological dope, Dr. Winslow. I'm listening. Tell me about this book deal."

Defeated, knowing she had no other choice, Jamie began. "All right. It was one of those dumb-luck things. Here I was, talking to some woman about my thesis, and suddenly, I have an agent *and* an incredible offer. It's big, Kell. I'm supposed to be some sort of phenomenon. A guru to the masses. Woman-to-woman sort of thing. And, yes, my research was sparked by our on-again off-again relationship, I admit it. But it's not about us directly. I couldn't tell you before because it's still confidential. I couldn't even tell Mom or Donna. There's a huge publicity campaign planned and the publisher doesn't want to get upstaged by anyone else before it gets off the ground."

Kell's handsome face was marred by a frown. "When's all this planned for?"

"Well, first I have to write the book. I've got three months to do that. And I expect the publicity will start a few months afterward. I don't really know, though." Sitting there, she wanted nothing more than to be able to get up and go to him, to be held in his arms, to feel safe. She feared, though, that would never again be possible. Her good luck could be the end of them. Talk about closure.

Kell broke into her sad reflections. "So what's this got to do with me? Who made you call me?"

"Dr. Hampton. He's my professor and mentor. And the one who holds my certification in his hands."

"Certification for what?"

"My license to practice. And the truth is...no license, no credentials. Which means no book deal."

"Which means no big bucks."

"Well, yes, but you don't have to make it sound so crass." Was it crass? She still worried about that. Maybe because it *had* all come so easily to her. There was a syndrome she knew of regarding new, young millionaires and their guilt over the easy wealth. Was that what she was suffering? Or was it something closer to home? "Still," she continued, "everything hinges on my being able to back up my book with professional credentials."

Kell stared at her as if she were some squishy gray thing that had just crawled out from under a rock. "Your license to practice. And this Dr. Hampton wanted you to call me because...?"

"Because I need closure. See, before licensing, I'm required to undergo a series of sessions myself. To make sure I'm grounded and well adjusted."

"Are you?"

"In some areas. Not so much where you're concerned. Which led Dr. Hampton to believe that we— you and I—have some unresolved issues between us. And he won't sign my certification until I...well, *we*...achieve closure."

Kell just stared at her, his dark eyes penetrating.

Jamie put a hand to her forehead. "God, it all sounds so, I don't know, calculating somehow, doesn't it?"

"Yes, it does." The detachment was still there in his

voice. "Does this professor know about the book deal?"

"No. Just my agent and the publisher. And now you."

"Interesting." He chuckled, humorlessly. "So the good doctor really threw a monkey wrench into the motor works when he wouldn't cooperate, didn't he? So I'm guessing you're here to achieve closure. That explains your opening line about us having to have sex. And your following it up with the act. Funny. I thought that's what women always accuse men of doing—solving everything with sex."

Jamie sprang to her feet. "I told you I was just teasing when I said that. I never meant for this afternoon to happen. It just *happened*, the same way it always does with us. But you make me sound cheap, like I'd have sex to secure a book deal."

"I didn't say it. You did. So tell me, Jamie, am I out of your system?"

Jamie gasped. Horrified and hurt, she turned her back to him. "Go to hell, Kellan Chance."

Too angry to cry, Jamie grabbed her purse and stalked to the front door. Wrenching it open, she turned to Kell and opened her mouth to speak, only, no words would come. Her gaze locked with his. Kell could have been chiseled out of marble, he was so cold, so still.

Something snapped inside Jamie. She wanted to hurt him right back. "Goodbye, Kell. I know it's not the first time you've heard that from me. But it is the last."

Kell took a step toward her, a fierce look on his face. "There never has been, and there never will be, a final goodbye between you and me, Jamie. You're only fooling yourself if you think otherwise." His expression intensified, became predatory...in a strangely sensual way. Like a taunt, a dare straight from the bedroom. "I'm in your blood, Jamie. I'm under your skin. Just like you are with me. So you can say goodbye all you want. But it won't last."

Jamie fought for breath. She had other things she wanted to say to Kell, but again no words would come. Somewhere deep inside her, she knew he was right. It wasn't over. And it probably never would be.

# 5

STANDING ON A DOORSTEP two days later and already asking himself why he'd thought this was a good idea, Kell rang the doorbell on the tile-roofed Camden residence nestled amongst the well-tended lawns and the waving palm trees of the Officers' Housing Area on MacDill Air Force Base.

The door opened. There stood Melanie Camden, dressed in peach capri pants and a matching halter top. It was the damnedest thing to Kell. Here she was a red-headed goddess turned loose on earth, yet he could only think of her as a friend. And then there was Jamie, pretty in a girl-next-door sort of way—yet he had the constant hots for her. Go figure.

Melanie's beautiful face lit with pleasure when she saw him. "Why, Kellan Chance. What a nice surprise. Come in." Her soft Southern voice and her genuine happiness at seeing him were everything Kell needed today.

Kell stepped over the threshold and stood in the tiled foyer, grateful for the air-conditioned coolness that surrounded him in the impeccably decorated quarters. "Hi, Melanie. Heard anything from Jeff?"

She closed the door and leaned her back against a wall, crossing her arms over her chest. "As a matter of fact, I have," she said brightly. "I just talked to him a bit ago. He still sounds so weak, but the doctors are telling him he's going to be absolutely a hundred percent in several months' time."

Relief washed over Kell. "Oh, hell, Melanie, that's fabulous news."

"Isn't it? In fact, he's well enough now that they're flying him home tomorrow. I wish I'd known that last weekend. I wouldn't have come back when I did. But still, I can hardly wait." Suddenly she sobered and leaned forward, putting her hand on his arm. "Kell, he had a message for you. He said to tell you this wasn't your fault. He doesn't blame you. Nobody does."

Kell drew in a deep breath. The guilt ate at him again. "That's pretty big of him. And it may even be true, but I can't help blaming myself anyway. I was the commander. Win or lose, it comes down on my head."

Melanie patted his arm. "I know. But I just hate it, Kell. It's so unfair." Her expression changed to one of concern. "So, what are they going to do to you? Have you heard anything?"

He exhaled and shrugged, trying to act as if it were no big deal. "Oh, yeah, I've heard. I was at HQ earlier today for further debriefing. Afterward, I went home but couldn't stand myself and my place, Melanie, so I changed out of my uniform and here I am. I hope it's okay?"

"You poor thing. You know it is. In fact, I'm about sick of being by myself here, too. I tell you what, you can stay for supper if you'll tell me what it is you aren't telling me."

Kell frowned. "Not telling you? What do you mean?"

"Oh, please. There's something eating at you, Kell. What is it?"

He ran a hand through his hair. "You're tough, you know that? But thanks for the supper invitation. I accept. And you might as well know the whole story. I'm looking at a desk job, Melanie. At Special Ops. A damn desk job."

Sympathy edged her eyes. "Oh, no. They can't make a desk jockey out of you. You'll just die—" She covered her mouth with her fingertips and stared wide-eyed at him. She lowered her hand. "I am so sorry. I didn't mean to say that. I could just bite my tongue."

"Forget it. You didn't say anything I didn't already know."

"Well, still, I shouldn't have said it. Of course you won't die. You'll be just fine." She gestured toward the kitchen. "You want some iced tea or a beer?"

"Tea's fine."

"Good. I'll get us both some." She turned around and walked away, calling out behind her, "Why don't you come in here with me. I'll take some steaks out, and we can talk. Anything else going on with you? How's your leg?"

Following behind her as ordered, and wondering why it was that he found her so easy to talk to when he didn't normally open up to anyone, Kell answered, "It's fine. The stitches come out in a few days. It's my head that's messed up now."

"Well, I expect so, what with everything that's happened recently." Now in the kitchen, Melanie motioned him to a bar stool on the other side of the breakfast bar. Kell sat down and rested his elbows on the counter. As Melanie set about opening cabinets and pulling out two tall tumblers, Kell began to feel better. He'd been right to come here. Melanie was such a good friend.

As if she'd heard his thoughts, she said, "So tell Melanie all about it, sugar. And I mean what *really* brought you here. There's more, isn't there?"

Bemused, Kell shook his head. "I give up. Yes, there's more. But it's got nothing to do with the mission. I'm resigned to that and the desk job. What's done is done. Instead, I need to talk to you about...Jamie Winslow."

Melanie whirled around, a glass in one hand, an ice cube in the other. "I just knew it. Why, as I live and breathe, Kellan Chance, you're here for girl talk, aren't you? Tell me, honey, what's happened?"

Suddenly Kell wasn't so sure he wanted to tell her. Guys didn't engage in...he winced...girl talk. "It's long and drawn out," he said, hedging.

"Well, of course it is. That's because it's about a woman." Raising her eyebrows archly, Melanie dropped the ice cube into the glass. "We are complicated creatures, darlin'. But, lucky for you, I have all the time in the world. Don't chicken out now."

Kell pulled back, not sure if he was insulted or amused. "I never chickened out on anything in my life. But you're right. Okay, to make a long story short, she came over—"

"She did? To your place?" Melanie's eyes were bright with delicious curiosity. Her Southern accent fairly dripped molasses. "When was this?"

Kell could see this wasn't going to be easy. Women

wanted every detail. "Two days ago. Monday. About 3:00 p.m."

"What was she wearing?"

"Clothes, Melanie. I don't know. Shorts and a blouse. Sandals."

"See? You did know."

"All right, I did. Anyway, she came over with some story about being worried about me and about needing closure before she could get her license to practice and...well, there's more but she asked me not to tell anybody else. It has to do with her career."

"Well, honey, skip the parts you can't tell me. I want the juicy stuff, anyway. The stuff that happened once you had her in your hot little clutches inside that wild bachelor pad of yours."

Kell grinned and shook his head in amused disbelief. "Melanie, have you ever considered writing for those soap operas you love? You'd be great at it. My 'wild bachelor pad'? Where'd you get that?"

"Oh, like you're a monk. Look at you, sweetheart. How *do* you keep the women off you?"

Kell made a broad gesture and looked down at himself. "Do you see any women here?"

Melanie shook her head. "That's beside the point. Spill your guts, honey."

Feeling embarrassment climb up his neck and face, Kell looked away from her, not knowing exactly how to proceed or whether he even should. But he knew he would. He could deny Melanie nothing. He owed her, the way he saw it. Her husband was shot up and in the hospital because of him. The least he could do was answer her questions. Besides, she was so relentless that somehow she got everything out of him anyway. And the truth was, he needed someone to talk to right now. "We...well, we ended up in bed."

Melanie slumped dramatically against the refrigerator. "Oh, I just knew it. The romance of it all." She put a hand to her chest. "I need to catch my breath."

Kell chuckled. "Knock it off, Melanie. Jeff's been gone too long."

Melanie stood up straight. "Honey, you got that right. That man needs to hurry up and get well." She pulled a pitcher of iced tea out of the refrigerator and walked over to Kell. "But we were talking about you and Miss Winslow." She handed him his glass. "Here you go. Now, do I hear wedding bells in the near future?"

Kell took a welcome swig from his glass. His throat was suddenly dry. "Not even close. We had a fight and she left."

Melanie's eyes widened. "I have got to sit down." She pulled out the other bar stool. "What in the world did you fight about, Kell?"

What could he say? That he'd accused her of using him and sex to secure her book deal? "Well, I can't really say..."

"I see. Well, no matter what you said to her, you were obviously wrong. You need to make it up to her."

Kell couldn't believe this. "Why do I have to be the one who was wrong?"

"Because you're the man, sweetie. Men always do something."

"I *said* something. You women always stick together, no matter what."

"Yes, we do. And that's because we know you men. Now, what are you going to do about Miss Winslow?"

"Nothing. It's over."

"I've heard this before—and about this same woman. Now, tell me this...are you sorry for what you said to her?"

"Yes." Kell hung his head, feeling as if he were ten years old again and was standing in front of his mother, who'd just got caught him beating up on T.J.

"Well then, if you're sorry, you need to tell her that."

Kell looked up at Melanie, ready to protest. But she had an eyebrow arched in such a way that said he'd better not disobey her. Besides, he really *was* sorry. "Well, I guess I *could* call her."

Melanie smiled...but shook her head. "You are so precious. No, you can't call her, honey. But you can go see her and apologize in person. And you can also take her a big old bunch of pretty-smelling flowers and a nice card. And then, you can only pray the woman will forgive you."

Kell could just see that scenario—him standing there with flowers and his heart in his hands. Pathetic. He shook his head. "I don't think so. Why would I do that?"

Melanie was undaunted. "For lots of reasons." She ticked them off on her fingers. "Because you were wrong. Because you love her. Because you need her to be your best friend and not me. And because it's eating you up to have her mad at you."

Kell pulled back to stare at her. "What makes you think that?"

Melanie put her hand on his arm. Her expression

was sympathetic. "Just looking at you, you poor thing. You haven't shaved. Your clothes are wrinkled. You look like you've lost weight. Honey, you've even got dark circles under your eyes. Now, you know I love you, but you look like hell. You're going to go home, get some sleep, and then tomorrow, you're going to go get that woman to forgive you."

"Like hell, Melanie. I can't—"

"Yes, you can. If you don't, at this rate, sweetie, you're going to be in the hospital bed next to Jeff's. And I simply won't have that. Do you hear me?"

KELL HAD INDEED heard Melanie—and took her advice the very next afternoon, although he still couldn't believe he was doing this. There he stood, in the carpeted hallway outside Jamie's apartment door. He was clean-shaven, his hair was freshly cut and his khaki pants and chambray shirt were ironed to such a degree he could have passed military inspection. In one hand he held flowers—a big old bunch of pretty-smelling ones, as Melanie had put it—in his other a mushy please-forgive-me card. What more proof did he need that the failed SEAL mission had injured more than his leg? If he had any sense left at all, he'd leave before Jamie—

The door in front of him opened, startling him—as well as Jamie, who gasped and stared at him wide-eyed. "Kellan David Chance. You startled the life out of me."

Remembering his mission, Kell answered suavely, "That's fair, because you take my breath away."

He had no idea where those words had come from, but they worked their magic. Awareness and hunger sparked in Jamie's blue eyes...and more. So much more. "I didn't...expect to see you today."

"I'm sure you didn't." And still he couldn't get enough of looking at her. All he'd ever wanted was right there in front of him. He wanted to hold her up against the wall, to lean in to her...kiss her...touch her...

"Kell?" He jerked out of his sensual reverie. "How'd you get inside the building?" Jamie asked. "I'm ten floors up, and my entry buzzer didn't ring."

"I slipped in behind a few people who were leaving." He couldn't believe he could talk so casually. Because he felt anything but casual around her. Already, his blood seemed to have thickened to the consistency of tar. This was nothing new. He knew exactly what was wrong with him—Jamie's nearness. She had always affected him this way.

"Well, that's great. So much for the security I pay for."

"Don't be too hard on your superintendent. Covert actions are what I do for a living, remember."

"Well, obviously. I mean...here you are." Her expression was expectant. Clearly, she was waiting for him to explain his presence.

And he was going to do just that, too, as soon as he finished taking in his fill of her. She was utterly gorgeous. Tanned, shapely. Her dark hair fell like a silky waterfall around her shoulders. He wanted to kiss her...all over. She had her purse and keys in her hand. He could probably kiss them, too. Suddenly, the situation dawned on him. "You getting ready to go out?"

"There's just no getting anything past you, is there?"

The honeymoon was over. She'd obviously remembered she was mad at him. But what exactly had he expected—another offer of sex? That damn Melanie had gotten him into this. "You're still mad, aren't you?"

"Yes." Jamie hadn't stepped out into the hall, nor had she asked him inside. She stood with her hand on the doorknob. "I have a right to be. You said some pretty awful things to me, Kellan."

"I know. That's why I brought these." He shoved the flowers and the card at her. "To help me say I'm sorry and that on a scale of one to ten, I'm lower than pond scum. Forgive me?" He tried a grin and a bit of levity for good measure. "Please don't pepper-spray me. I hate that."

Despite herself, Jamie shook her head and finally chuckled, taking the flowers and the card he offered. "These are beautiful, thank you. And you are absolutely pathetic, do you know that?"

"Yes, I do. But I figured I was either way."

"Either way? What do you mean?"

"Melanie told me yesterday that I was pathetic if I *didn't* come over here and beg your forgiveness."

Jamie'd been smelling the flowers and smiling her pleasure, but now her grin faded. "Oh, really? Melanie from the airport?" Kell nodded. "You...talked to her about us?"

Almost too late, he saw the yawning trap before him. He'd already stuck his foot squarely in the middle of it, but he didn't see the sense in springing the trigger mechanism. "Only a little bit. All I said was I had behaved like an ass and you were angry at me. Deservedly so."

Jamie's eyes widened. "Oh?"

It was getting worse...like a runaway train. "Yes. And she told me I looked like hell and that I had to come tell you I was sorry. So here I am...and I'm sorry, Jamie. Sincerely sorry."

She ignored his apology. "Would you be here now if Melanie hadn't made you?"

"She didn't make me." Kell frowned at Jamie's implication. "No one makes me do anything. She *advised* me. And I thought she was right."

Jamie narrowed her eyes. "You didn't answer my question."

"Damn, Jamie, cut me some slack, okay? What difference does it make? I'm here, aren't I? And I'm apologizing. Doesn't that count for something?"

Jamie relaxed her posture, obviously relenting a bit. "You're right. I'm sorry. But I have to know...did you tell her about the book deal?"

He exhaled sharply. "No, Jamie. I violated no confidences."

"Good. What about us sleeping together?"

Obviously the interrogation was going to continue until she was satisfied. But that didn't stop Kell from grinning and purposely misunderstanding her question. "Oh, I'm still all for that." When she bristled, he added, "Hold on, I'm just teasing you. But, yes, I did tell her about the two of us."

Jamie carefully, deliberately put the flowers on a table inside her door. The unopened card followed.

Kell watched her dismissive actions, thinking of all the time and thought he'd put into selecting his gifts. No way was he going to allow her to just set them aside. He pointed at the card. "You ought to open that. There might be money inside."

"You put *money* in the card?"

Now he heard how that sounded. Yesterday...sex. Today...money. "No. Of course not. It was a bad joke." Silence. "Forget it."

Jamie poked out her bottom lip. "What else did you tell Melanie?"

Wearied of this line of questioning, Kell exhaled. "Jamie, look, I have found myself in obscure foreign countries in the middle of big fields that were riddled with land mines. Successfully navigating through them was less treacherous than this conversation is."

Jamie's expression softened. "I'm sorry, Kell. You're right. I think the whole Melanie thing threw me. She's just so gorgeous and that's intimidating. And to know you talked to her about us...well, I—"

"Hey, worry less about her and think of me, okay? Melanie's a friend, a good friend. That's all. And I'm trying to be nice here. Hell, I even got a haircut. I don't know what else to do. If you can't forgive me, then I'll just...go away."

She reached out to him. "Please don't go away."

"I don't want to. But I don't know what else to do. All I want is another chance. Just tell me what I have to do to be forgiven. I'll do anything."

She'd listened quietly, but now she raised an eyebrow. Then her expression brightened. "Do you mean that? Anything?"

He was a dead man. The sinking feeling in the pit of his stomach attested to it. "I don't like that look. I'm betting that whatever you're thinking doesn't have anything to do with door-to-door sex."

"You're right. It doesn't." Now clearly a woman on a mission, Jamie nimbly stepped outside her apartment, closed the door and locked it behind her. She zipped around to face Kell. Her face was alight with glee. "You're going to go to Dr. Hampton's office with me."

The name rang a bell. Kell frowned. "Refresh my memory. Who is Dr. Hampton?"

"My shrink. Or counselor. Professor. Whatever. The man who's holding my life hostage because he won't sign a simple piece of paper allowing me to practice psychology and make a fortune. Anyway, you're going to go with me this afternoon—that's where I was headed—and you're going to tell him that we have finally achieved closure—"

"We have?"

"Of course we have, silly." She leaned in to him and lightly kissed him on the lips. "You're forgiven, by the way."

"Well, good. But I don't know, Jamie—"

She put her hand on her hip.

She was right. What did it matter if he didn't understand the concept of closure? She was the professional here. He threw his hands up. "All right. I give. Closure it is. Lead the way, my friend."

Jamie brightened, and launched herself into his arms, planting kisses all over his face. "Oh, Kell, thank you. This means so much to me. I love you."

Kell held her tight and tried to get in a few kisses and words of his own. "I love you, too, Jamie. You're welcome."

He just hoped she wouldn't mind if he asked the good Dr. Hampton a few questions of his own about the nature of closure. Just to be sure.

## 6

JAMIE COULD HAVE cheerfully choked the life out of Kellan Chance—even if she'd have to spend the rest of her life in prison. Even the specter of incarceration and a chain-gang existence couldn't deter her from her death wish for the man. There they'd been, innocently sitting side by side on the couch in Dr. Hampton's inner office, with her blithely telling Dr. Hampton that she and Kell had achieved closure, when suddenly Kell had said he had some questions.

Talk about betrayal. *No wonder I have problems with commitment.* Jamie crossed her arms over her chest and silently fumed as the men talked about her as if she weren't there. And she couldn't do a thing about it, either! After all, she was the one who'd asked Dr. Hampton if Kell could sit in on her session. She was the one who'd told him that Kell had something important to say. And she was the one who'd been royally set up. *Never trust a SEAL.* That was her new motto.

"So, Dr. Hampton," Kell asked, "what's a good working definition of *closure?* I'm not sure Jamie has ever really given me one. So how can I say for sure that we have it if I don't know what it is?"

"Point taken." Dr. Hampton stroked his beard and nodded. "*Closure.* Let me see if I can put it in lay terms, Commander Chance. I suppose you'd say it was an end point, really. It's not about happy or unhappy endings. What it *is* about is closing a door on a situation or a relationship in such a way that you can peacefully live with it. It's an acknowledgment that something or even someone didn't turn out how you'd have liked, but you know you did everything you could do to affect a good outcome. It's knowing that you're okay with the situation and can move on."

"Hmm," Kell said thoughtfully. "So, basically, it's about letting go?"

"That's an excellent way of putting it. It's essentially living with the realization that not all relationships are going to be as you'd have them. But it goes beyond that, too. Because it's not a closure until *you* can truly live with the situation or the decision of another."

"I see. Until I can sleep at night without drugs and then face myself in the mirror every day when I shave."

"Uh, well, yes, that's one way of putting it, Commander. You're a very astute thinker."

Jamie rolled her eyes. *Oh, please. The Mutual Admiration Society meeting will now come to order.* She glared at Kell, only to see him staring...and grinning...right back at her. It took every adult instinct Jamie possessed not to stick her tongue out at him.

Kell chuckled, then turned to face Dr. Hampton. "Thank you, Dr. Hampton. I appreciate the explanation. Unfortunately, though, I have to admit that Jamie and I aren't anywhere near having closure. Not yet."

Jamie gasped, grabbing Kell's shirtsleeve. "Of course we are, Kellan Chance. I'm over you." She poked him with her finger, then looked at Dr. Hampton. "Really, I am!"

Dr. Hampton shifted in his leather-upholstered chair as if he was uncomfortable. He kept looking at Jamie as if he'd never met her before and was a bit alarmed by the desperation she was displaying.

Jamie rushed on. "He's just angry because I'm over him. He even accused me of having sex with him to get him to come here and say we have achieved closure."

Dr. Hampton's eyes rounded as he looked from her...to Kell, who nodded...and back to her. "If that's true, then this is a very serious charge, Jamie. And extremely unethical on your part."

Jamie froze...and then began perspiring. She hadn't thought of her bright idea to bring Kell here today for a quick fix to her licensing dilemma in those terms. But now she could see that was exactly what she'd done—jeopardized her career by holding her forgiveness over Kell's head in exchange for getting him to lie for her. She hung her head. She didn't deserve to be in practice. Knowing what she had to do, she opened her mouth to confess—but Kell jumped in first.

"That's not it Dr. Hampton. The sex was three days ago and had nothing to do with today. She was right to be angry about the things I said to her. In fact, it wasn't until I went over to her place today that she invited me to come with her today."

"Kell," Jamie said quietly. "You're lying and you know it. What I did was despicable and I should pay for it."

Kell took Jamie's hands in his. "You're not despicable, Jamie you're the most honorable person I know. *I* was the one out of line, not you."

She couldn't have loved him more than she did at this moment. But neither could she allow him to compromise himself. Kell believed in duty and honor. This would cost him heavily consciencewise and it was up to her to make things right. "But, Kell, I did ask you to come here today to say we had achieved closure."

He nodded. "You did. And I came because I thought, at that time, that we did have closure. But then Dr. Hampton defined the concept for me. And then I realized that maybe we really didn't have it. So, see? You didn't lie. I just changed my mind."

"You did not." Jamie glanced down at her hands, held tightly in his. It looked so right. And yet, everything else was so wrong. When had it ever been any different? "You're just trying to protect me."

Kell released her hands and gently raised her chin. His dark eyes were clear, his voice unwavering in its sincerity. "I'm not lying."

Jamie felt she didn't deserve this man. "You are. I know you, and I can tell."

Kell sat back. "I'm not so sure you *do* know me, Jamie. I've changed."

"You keep saying that, but I don't see how."

"You don't? Well, I have a desk job now at the base. I'm not putting my life on the line anymore. That's a major change."

A shocking one, too. "A desk job? Why do you have a desk job?"

He shrugged. "All I can say is that it has something to do with how I was wounded. And here's another way I've changed. I'm here with you now in a psychologist's office, trying to come to some kind of understanding about our relationship. That's another change."

It was, and she was forced to concede as much. "You're right. You'd always said therapy was just a bunch of psycho mumbo jumbo."

Dr. Hampton cleared his throat. "Excuse me, if I may break in at this point...with a bit of, uh, psycho mumbo jumbo?"

Jamie had forgotten the doctor was in the room.

When they turned to look at him, Dr. Hampton said, "Thank you. May I just say that the two of you behave as if you've been married for ten years? And I'm not so sure I mean that totally in a bad way. But my comment speaks to the obvious, the years of intimacy and caring—and disagreements—between the two of you that keep you at odds with each other, unable to resolve your differences."

Hearing the note of censure in his voice, despite his somewhat reassuring assessment, Jamie sat quietly looking down at her lap. Could this be worse? She glanced up at Kell. He looked as guilty as she felt, but his expression was also tinged with little-boy belligerence. He looked so endearing, that it was hard for her not to laugh. She firmed her lips together and bit down on the inside of her cheek, believing that to laugh now would certainly end her career before it ever got off the ground.

"Well, then, having said that," Dr. Hampton said into the silence, "allow me also to say that I am just going to forget what you told me about the circumstances that brought you both here today. Instead, I'd like to focus on what I've been hearing. We've got something to build with here. You two obviously care very much for each other, but are no closer to closure than China is geographically to North Dakota. So here's my proposal."

Dr. Hampton took a breath and consulted his notes. Jamie couldn't help feeling a thrill, hearing his assessment that she and Kell cared very much for each other. It was that obvious to a third party? That had to mean something. She exchanged a here-we-go glance with Kell and then looked at Dr. Hampton.

"I'll start with you, Jamie. You still have a fair amount of time left to clear this situation up."

She nodded. Then Kell cut in. "And I'm already on a thirty-day leave, sir."

"Yes, you mentioned a wound of some sort. I assume you're all right?"

He shrugged. "Yeah. It was a line-of-duty thing."

"I understand. Still, it's very generous of you, Commander Chance, to give of your time." Dr. Hampton then addressed them both. "What I want you to do in the time that remains to you, if you'll both agree, is to behave differently toward each other. And by that, I mean you are to proceed as if you have no past together. As if you'd never met before now, this very minute, right here in my office."

Jamie frowned, not sure where he was going with this. "You mean like strangers? I don't see how that would help us resolve our past issues."

"Let me finish. After everything I've just observed, I now believe your only chance at some sort of closure that is acceptable to you both is if you *do* remain in each other's lives. Am I right?"

Jamie wanted to jump up and yell that yes he was right, but she wasn't about to do that if Kell didn't feel the same way. She looked at him. He was looking at her. His dark eyes met hers and held. Neither one spoke.

"I see no one wishes to contradict me," Dr. Hampton said, amusement in his voice. "Therefore, I shall proceed. I'm beginning to think the reason you two can't achieve any kind of closure is because you're victims of that old saying 'Can't live with him, can't live without him.' And why? Because, I believe, you continue to behave toward each other exactly the way you always have. You won't allow the other one to be different. And can't trust that the other one actually may have changed. Are we in agreement so far?"

"I'm with you, Dr. Hampton," Kell said. He turned to Jamie, who couldn't believe this most reasonable of beings sitting next to her was the Kellan Chance she knew. "I think I get it, Jamie. I've only ever taken physical risks, as if putting my life on the line proves I'm alive. When in truth I'm only alive if I have you."

Tears rounded Jamie's eyes. "Do you know how long I've waited to hear you say that, Kell? To know that you'd realize how precious you are to me and how I need you safe and by my side?"

Kell reached over to clasp her hand. Thus encouraged, Jamie looked to Dr. Hampton. "All right, apparently we're going to try to make this work. How do we go about this plan of yours?"

"It's simple, actually. You need to retrace your steps

through all the stages of your relationship. The first one is a rekindling of your friendship, a rediscovery and acknowledgment of the other one's traits that you admire. From there, you start to date. But you'll do it as two people who've only just met," Dr. Hampton informed them. "In other words, you can bring up no recriminations about past behaviors or failed attempts at a relationship because you never had one."

"Sounds like...fun," Kell said, grimacing slightly.

Jamie darted a glance his way, wondering if he was pulling back because of the warm, intense things he'd just said to her. He had to be as startled as she was that he'd revealed such personal insight. The poor guy. He'd probably never really questioned himself or his behavior before now. These new feelings had to be unsettling.

Jamie sent him a warm smile of understanding. But Kell avoided her eyes. Jamie took a deep resolute breath and faced her therapist. "I agree with Kell. It sounds like fun. And I think it's worth a try."

Dr. Hampton's eyes lit with pleasure. "Good. This is a perfect opportunity to find out if you would have been compatible if you'd never met until now."

The psychologist/researcher in Jamie began to get interested. "But we'll still bring our personalities and our old fears into this new relationship. How do we handle all that?"

Kell sat forward, resting his elbows on his knees and folding his hands together. "I was wondering the same thing."

Dr. Hampton nodded. "I understand that this will be a bit false, given that you're both shaped by your past relationships with each other. And it may not work...but maybe try this. Pretend that you had those relationships with other people and not each other."

Jamie sat up straight. "That's brilliant, Dr. Hampton. Then we should be able to listen more objectively to each other if we take our hurt feelings out of the picture." She beamed at Kell. "This could work. We wouldn't have anything to be defensive about."

Kell sat back and frowned. "Sort of like listening to each other gripe about someone else, right, Dr. Hampton?"

"Essentially. But I prefer the word *evaluate* over *gripe*. So, do you think this is something you can do?"

Dr. Hampton was looking at Kell. Jamie held her breath, waiting for his answer. She figured her mentor assumed she'd go along with the idea because...what choice did she have?

Kell nodded slowly. "I'll give it a whirl. Still, I'm starting to feel like a guinea pig."

"You might be. But only with your own feelings. This is a common concern raised by couples who've known each other since they were mere children. 'Would we have fallen in love if we'd met when we were older and therefore were different people?' they always wonder. I will admit, it's an intriguing angle."

Jamie found it hard to contain her growing enthusiasm. "I really like this. It's exciting." Then she caught Kell's smug expression. Her heart leaped. "The psychology aspects of it, Kell, are exciting. Don't go preening just yet."

He frowned. "I do not preen."

"Well then, here we go," Dr. Hampton said loudly,

obviously jumping in before another round of squabbling could fire up. He stood up and indicated for them to do the same. Then he performed an introduction ceremony. "Lieutenant Commander Kellan Chance, it is my pleasure to introduce you to Dr. Jamie Winslow, Ph.D. Jamie, this is Kellan. Kellan...Jamie. Now, shake hands...and *don't* come out fighting."

THE GRAND EXPERIMENT hit a snag within ten minutes. Kell was standing outside the glass-and-steel high-rise building that housed Dr. Hampton's office, Jamie at his side. Traffic chugged by on Kennedy Boulevard. The day was inexcusably hot and beautiful. To each side of the double-wide glass doors behind them, a tall hedge of blooming gardenias filled the air with their sweet and cloying scent. People, intent on their own business, swarmed around them.

But Kell and Jamie were intent only on each other. They were arguing.

Kell stood like a boulder in the midst of the busy stream of humanity flowing past them. His arms were crossed, and he was frowning. "I still can't believe you used your cell phone to call a cab. I drove you here, and I'll give you a ride home."

"Sorry, Kell, I can't. I wouldn't get in the car of a man I'd just met. You should know that."

"How? I'm the man you just met, remember?" Already hating Dr. Hampton's stupid idea, Kell let out an exasperated breath. "Come on, Jamie, be reasonable. Let me give you a ride home and then I'll call you and ask you out. We can set up a date and go from there like we just met."

Jamie crossed her arms. "Excuse me? What happened to the friendship stage? The just-liking-each-other part?"

"We can't do that if we're not together, right? Besides, I already like you. And you like me. So let's go out to dinner."

"Listen to you, you smug thing. How do you know I'll say yes? *And*...how do you know I won't call *you* first and ask you out?"

"Because you've never done that before."

She grinned. "Gotcha. How do you know what I've done before? For all you know, I could be a nun or a nudie-bar dancer."

Kell could only stare at the sweet face of the woman who excited—and frustrated—the hell out of him. Just the sight of her made his pulse pick up its pace. For some reason, she alone fired his jets. "I don't think you'd be asking me out if you were a nun, Jamie."

"That's true. Bad example. But would you go out with me if I danced in nudie bars?"

Kell grinned. "You don't know much about men, do you, Dr. Winslow? Hell, yes, I would. You'd make a great nude dancer. You certainly have the attributes."

She pursed her lips. "Just never mind my attributes, mister. Another crack like that and I may not want to call you."

Kell grinned and leaned in toward her, lowering his voice. "Why? Because I said you have a nice body? You do. I've seen it."

Fighting a grin, she pushed him back. "You have not. We just met."

"Oh. Right." Kell realized he was suddenly excited

by the prospect of *not* knowing how Jamie would react, and of learning every new thing about her. He'd been right earlier—this could be fun. Safe and kinky fun. He crossed his arms and looked at her assessingly. "Say you do call me and ask me out. How do you know *I'll* accept?"

Awareness flared in Jamie's blue eyes. "Well, I don't know, do I? Guess I'll just have to call to find out."

Watching her warmed Kell considerably. Could it be that she, too, had suddenly realized the sensual possibilities of this charade, this thrill of the unknown they were engaging in? A flutter in his belly had Kell feeling suddenly edgy. Suddenly, he couldn't wait to get to know her. Beyond that, he couldn't wait to pursue her...or to allow her to pursue him, as the case may be. "This is going to be fun, Jamie. Big fun."

She turned that grin loose and beamed. "I can't wait to get home to see who calls the other one first."

"Well, here, let me make it simple for you. You call me. I love being pursued."

Jamie looked at him questioningly. "You do? I didn't know that about you."

Kell shrugged. "There're a lot of things you don't know about me, Dr. Winslow."

Her grin was back. "You can call me Jamie."

"Thanks." He stuck his hand out. "Hi, Jamie. You can call me Kell."

Jamie slipped her hand into his. Kell—overcome with joy at this chance of a new beginning with her—exuberantly tugged her into his embrace and swung her around. Jamie clung tightly to him and laughed her pleasure. Then Kell put her down, and ignoring startled passersby, he held Jamie out from him and looked down into her sweet, sexy face. "This is going to be great, Jamie. I haven't felt this good in a long time."

"Me, neither. It seems so positive, Kell. Finally. I'm so glad all our emotional baggage won't be in the way." Then, without warning, she did a one-eighty, becoming the seductress. She trailed a finger down his chest, and her voice was a purr that made Kell shiver where he stood. "But there is one thing you should know about me right up front, Mr. Kellan Chance."

Under her spell, Kell tensed with desire. "Only one? All right, what is it?"

Leaning into him, Jamie looked up at him through her long, dark eyelashes. "I don't go to bed on a first date."

Pretending to be crestfallen, Kell let go of her and took a step back. He held his hands up, signaling a halt. "There's a problem. I do."

Jamie advanced on him and swatted playfully at his arm. "You little tramp. You do not."

He chuckled. "I can't believe you called me a tramp. But how do you—a new acquaintance of mine—know I don't put out on a first date?"

Jamie silently considered him, sending him a sidelong glance. "You're right. I don't. But, there's only one way for me to find out, isn't there?"

Kell favored her with his best suggestive grin. "That's the way I see it."

Just then, a cab pulled up in front of them. Jamie hailed the driver and then turned to Kell. "Well, my ride's here. It was nice meeting you."

Kell chuckled. "The pleasure was all mine." And it

was. He couldn't believe it. He was giddy with excitement. It was like...*bam! Love at first sight.* "All right. Here we go." He opened the back door of the cab and helped her in.

"Thank you. You're such a gentleman," she said from the back seat.

Kell shrugged away the compliment. "I try to make my mother proud."

Jamie shook her head with a smile. Then she gave the driver her address and asked him to wait a moment. She turned to Kell. "So, can I call you sometime?"

Clutching the cab's open back door with one hand, Kell draped himself in the opening and leaned over to see her. "Sure. I'd like that."

"Great. What's your phone number?"

Kell closed the cab door. Jamie rolled her window down and looked expectantly at him. "It's in the book," he said, winking at her before he turned to swagger away, triumphant, toward the parking garage.

But a feminine shout of appreciation... "Whoa, honey, I wish I had that swing in my backyard!" ...and a whistle halted Kell in his tracks. He whipped around to see the cab departing and Jamie leaning out the window, blowing kisses his way. Even the cabbie waved to him.

Embarrassment lit up Kell's face as people who were walking by grinned and blatantly assessed his qualifications. Mustering what was left of his dignity, Kell did an about-face and marched toward the parking garage. *Paybacks are hell, Dr. Winslow. Just wait until the next time I see you.*

He had every reason to believe it would be that same evening.

# 7

THREE DAYS LATER, they once again found themselves in bed. Dr. Hampton's grand experiment had failed—miserably.

"I can't believe you didn't call me for three days," Kell said, pouting. "I sat around the house all weekend long waiting for that damn phone to ring."

He was quite put out. Jamie stroked his arm. "Ah, you poor misused man. Don't you just hate it when that happens? I know we women do."

Kell narrowed his eyes. "So is that what the treatment was about? A retaliation against men who don't call?"

"No, of course not." Then she appeared to think about it. "Maybe. I don't know. But that's not a bad chapter heading. Chapter Two—Men Who Don't Call."

He pulled himself up on an elbow and stared at her. "You know, I'm beginning to think you're toying with my affections. First, we're friends. Then we date. I make embarrassing revelations about the state of my heart, prove to you how I've changed. Have I been set up?"

"Oh, Kell, I'd hoped you'd trust me more than that by now. No, you haven't been set up. Dr. Hampton's suggestion had nothing to do with my book. Think about it. My Ph.D. wouldn't have been conferred on me if I hadn't completed my thesis and my research. Besides, I couldn't change my research. That would be unethical. I have to write the book from the data I've collected—not from our dates."

Kell lowered his gaze contritely. "I guess I knew that. I didn't mean to accuse you of being unethical. I'm just paranoid. A hazard of my profession." Kell raised his head, staring up at her with dark, expressive eyes that never failed to excite her. Dreamy bedroom eyes, she'd once called them. "So, Jamie, is that what you've been doing for three days? Writing?"

"No." Guilt assailed her. Kell's expression was so sincere—and she wasn't. "But I have been pretty busy."

He let out a short grunt. "Great. You did everything else you had to do and then called me with the crumbs of time you had left over." He put his hand on his chest. "I feel so used."

And he should, Jamie thought. She couldn't look him in the eye right now. She hadn't called him because she'd thought it would be fun to be unpredictable and hard to get. She'd thought it would up the romance factor, make him think of her differently. Always before, she'd been at his beck and call. She'd allowed him to take her for granted, to become comfortable with her always being there. Well, no more, she'd told herself. She called it practice for when she was on tour once her book came out. For when *she* was the one who wasn't there.

That had sounded good in theory. But in actual practice? She'd hated every minute of her little experiment.

Not calling him, as he had expected her to do, had been the most excruciating thing she'd ever done. Or, not done, actually. It had taken the concerted efforts of her friends to get her through the past few days, too. She'd let Becca, Carrie and Jan in on what was going on with her and Kell. Agog with curiosity, they'd helped keep her strong. It was like being in training to become a new woman.

Still, only her girlfriends' combined willpower had stopped her from running like some world-class sprinter right to his door. Thank heaven for shopping sprees and credit cards and chocolate. Yesterday, Jan had to work, but Becca and Carrie had come over and they'd all three gone to a movie. That had been disastrous—a summer romantic comedy that had left Jamie wanting to throw herself in Kell's arms.

"You're awfully quiet, Jamie. Is there something you want to tell me? Have you changed your mind about this experiment of Dr. Hampton's?"

"Kell, we're in bed together. Naked. How can you think I've changed my mind?"

"I don't know." He picked at a thread in the sheet. "I thought maybe you were trying to give me a taste of my own medicine."

Jamie took his handsome face in her hands and kissed his forehead. "You are so cute. No. It wasn't revenge. I was just trying to be different, you know, not so predictable. But it didn't work. Obviously. Remember," she said with forced cheeriness, "all I said was that I'd call you *sometime*. I didn't say when. And while I'm flattered, I certainly didn't expect you to be sitting around pining for me. I figured you had a life."

"I do. And I don't pine. Men don't pine."

"They certainly do." Amused at his injured air, Jamie reached over and poked his arm. "You could have called me, you know."

"No, I couldn't. I was busy, too."

Feeling in control, Jamie ran her gaze over his handsome face, noting his hawkish nose, his high cheekbones...his firm and sensual lips. Despite the pricks of desire that assailed her, she managed to keep her voice light. "Busy doing what? I thought you were sitting around waiting on me to call."

He lowered his eyebrows. "Not every minute. I did go see my friend Jeff Camden yesterday."

Jamie quit playing with him. Genuine emotion backed her words. "Oh, that is such good news. He's back home, then?"

"He's home."

"Melanie must be so happy. How's Jeff doing?"

Kell shrugged. "Okay, I guess. He looks like hell."

He was hiding his feelings, Jamie knew. She allowed a thoughtful moment to pass. "And you think it's your fault, don't you?" she asked softly.

Kell gave her a sharp look. "Don't play psychologist with me, Jamie. I don't need my head examined."

Contrite, she looked down. "I'm sorry." Then she met his gaze, saw the glitter of defensiveness in his eyes. "I guess this whole conversation isn't one we should be having. It's not exactly in accordance with what Dr. Hampton wants us to do. I mean, if we'd just met, I wouldn't know anything about Jeff or the accident. And I wouldn't know how you'd feel about it, would I?"

"No." Kell shifted position. "You know what? This is a pain, trying to act like we've just met. I thought it would be fun the other day, but now I'm not so sure."

Jamie couldn't have agreed more, but she wanted to hear his reasoning. "What do you mean?"

"Well, there wasn't a thing wrong with the old Jamie. I miss her." His dark eyes met hers again, all traces of exasperation gone.

Touched by his words, Jamie melted. "What a sweet thing to say, Kell. I miss you, too."

"Yeah?" His voice was gruff now. "What was wrong with the new Kell?"

"Nothing." She grinned and smoothed her hand over his bare chest, noting the fine firmness of his muscles, the smooth texture of his skin...the way he sucked in his breath as she roved her hand over the sculpted plane of his chest. "I just don't know the new Kell, that's all. So I'm not comfortable with him yet."

Kell chuckled evilly. "You'd have a hard time making a jury believe that. I'm naked and in your bed—and have been for the past two hours."

Pretending shock, Jamie abruptly sat up. Her tangled hair fell around her face. She shoved it back. "I slept with the new Kell? I thought it was with the old Kell." She flopped back down on the tangled sheets. "Great. I put out on a first date. There goes my reputation. And our course of action with Dr. Hampton."

"Oh, the hell with Dr. Hampton. He can get his own girl." Kell gathered her in his arms and rolled on top of her. Jamie welcomed his weight. The feel of his hard-muscled body atop hers stirred the fires inside her that he'd only minutes ago banked with his lovemaking.

Staring down at her, he kissed the tip of her nose. "But don't worry, my friend. I'm not the kiss-and-tell type."

"Thank God. You know, I kind of like this new Kell."

"You do? Let's see if we can make you love him." He dipped his head and took her mouth in a kiss that ravaged Jamie's senses all the way to her curling toes.

His tongue plunged into her mouth, stealing the very breath from her...until she was whimpering. Kell pulled back and gently nipped and tugged at her lips. Then he peppered tiny biting kisses along her chin, her jaw. With a rumbling purr deep in her throat, Jamie dug her hands into his short hair and pulled his head down to hers once again. This time it was her kiss that left him breathless. She just couldn't get enough of him. She was insatiable where he, and only he, was concerned.

In no time at all, kissing and fondling weren't enough. Jamie raked her nails down Kell's back. With a cry, he arched over her and Jamie captured one of his nipples with her mouth. A strangling gurgle from him urged her on. Inflamed by his response to her touch, Jamie licked at his nipple and sucked, while kneading the muscles in his back. In no time his hips were arching against her...and she was responding in kind, thrusting upward.

"Damn, Jamie, you make me crazy," he muttered as he kissed her neck, her collarbone and slowly slid down her. "I lose control around you."

"Good," she murmured, holding his head as she directed him to her breast. "That's how I want you. I want you crazy for me, Kell."

"I am, baby, I am." With those words, his hot mouth closed over her nipple, wringing a cry out of Jamie. Her womb felt heavy, soft...open. With much the same motions he'd employed with her mouth when he'd kissed her, Kell swirled his tongue over her already stiff nipple, eliciting an erotic tingling that centered itself right in the middle of her. If he kept that up, she'd pass out. It was that simple. Just when she thought she couldn't stand the sensation a moment longer, Kell relented and kissed his way across her skin to her other breast. There he repeated his tender ministrations.

"Oh, Kell, I don't think I can take much more. I'm about to explode."

"Hmm, baby, then wait for me. Let me help you." He slid farther down her, his hands and his mouth never leaving her body. He positioned himself between her thighs and encouraged her to bend her knees. When she did, he lowered his head and took her into his mouth. The same swirling kiss that he'd lavished on her mouth and her breasts, he now centered on her very femininity.

Clutching at the covers, her eyes closed, her mouth open, Jamie writhed with the pleasure of what Kell was doing to her body. Her hips began an answering movement, rotating in time with each thrust of his tongue inside her. She couldn't talk. She could only utter sounds, nonsense syllables...and his name. The hot and tightening coil, with its honeyed wetness and the attendant lethargy in her legs, began. It rose like a cresting wave that had Jamie caught up in its swell. All she could do was cling to the bedding and hold her breath in joyous anticipation of the sensations that would rob her temporarily of coherence. And then...the moment arrived. Kell sensed it, too, because he held her tightly to him and ardently flicked his tongue over her exposed bud. He made a sound deep in his throat. The vibration of it put Jamie's body over the edge. She rode the undulating waves of fiery heat and pleasure until she could take no more.

"Oh, Kell," she cried out, completely wrung out with passion sated.

Kell relented, now softly kissing her mound and her inner thighs. Jamie opened her eyes and saw him pull up onto his knees. Her gaze locked with his. His breathing was every bit as labored as hers, she noticed. His cheeks were suffused with the blush of desire...and he was hard with wanting her. "You're beautiful, Jamie. So damn beautiful. When your body responds to me like that, I feel...I feel like—"

"I know." Jamie held her arms out to him. "You're good, Kell. My body loves you as much as I do. Come here."

And he did. Once again he settled on top of her, holding her and kissing her. Jamie returned ardor for ardor. The feel of his weight pressing into her, the scent of his skin...clean, fresh...the way he made love to her as much with his words as with his body inflamed Jamie even more. She shifted her hips and wrapped her legs around Kell's hips. "I need you, Kell."

Smiling seductively down at her, he took her mouth in another heated kiss and moved his hips until he was sliding...sliding...sleekly into her. A sigh of fulfillment escaped Jamie and was answered by Kell's. He ended their kiss at the same time he began the thrusting that never failed to drive Jamie wild. She wrapped her arms around his neck and whispered encouragement. And Kell, like a bull, pushed into her, holding her tightly to him, pounding, ardent, intent...driven. Jamie felt his hardness swell inside her. She knew his moment was close. A second later, he gasped and tensed over her. His thrusts intensified until they were almost a vibration inside her. Jamie immediately increased the pace of her movements against him. When he cried out and stilled, frozen atop her, Jamie was frenzied, helping him, aiding him...until she too exploded and her body took over, clutching at Kell's hardness with spasms born of pleasure. Together, they rode the wave that took them to paradise.

The moment seemed to last forever and yet not hardly long enough. He collapsed on top of her, his face resting next to hers on the bed. A fine sheen of perspiration coated Jamie's skin, as it did Kell's. She relaxed her legs and lay contentedly under him, stroking the nape of his neck. After a few silent moments with only their hard breathing to punctuate the passing seconds, Kell managed to raise himself up and look down at her. He smiled.

"I have a question for you, Dr. Winslow. Seeing how good this feels, why don't people spend all their time doing this?"

Jamie again wrapped her arms around his neck. "I don't know, Commander Chance. Maybe because they'd die of the pleasure."

He nodded. "And maybe because they'd wear certain body parts down to nubs. And that wouldn't be funny."

Jamie chuckled, forgetting he was still inside her. He tensed and pulled out. He looked so offended. Jamie loved it. "Sorry. But you're the one who made me laugh."

"Teach me, won't it?" He leered at her. "It felt kind of good, actually. I love it when your body closes around me."

Jamie shook her head in mock censure. "Stop it. Or you'll end up with only that nub you're so worried about."

"Okay. You know, I don't think I can take much more of this closure, Jamie. It's about to kill me."

Jamie pulled herself up on her elbows, tossing her head back to get her hair out of her eyes. "Don't mistake this for closure, Kell. It's not even close. You know—" she paused, frowning "—an awful thing has just occurred to me. Sex may be our problem. It may be what keeps us from coming to some sort of long-term resolution between us."

"You're wrong. Sex is never a problem." Kell's expression indicated he thought she'd spoken blasphemy. He pointed at her. "You're very, very wrong, young lady. And you are never to say that again."

She couldn't help but laugh. "You know, it's hard to be serious with you sitting there like some ancient fertility god." Jamie sat up and scooted to the edge of the bed. "Let's get dressed. I think we need to talk."

Kell pitched forward on the bed and lay there, facedown. "Not 'we need to talk,'" he moaned. "I hate that almost as much as I do the word *closure*."

Jamie stood up and, for a moment, marveled at having a gorgeous man like Kell in her bed—and in her life. On an impulse, she went over and kissed him in the small of his back. "Come on," she encouraged, giving his firm buttock an appreciative pat. "It won't be so awful."

IT WAS, though. It was terrible. They'd been doing so well together earlier...and then had come The Talk. After this, Kell promised himself that he'd never again talk with a psychologist about sex. Because what Jamie was saying was...there would be no more sex.

"Not even if we get married?"

"Kell, be serious."

They were fully clothed and sitting in the tastefully decorated living room of Jamie's condo on Bayshore Boulevard. Kell leaned forward to retrieve his beer. Taking a sip, he looked over at Jamie, seeing her troubled eyes and hating that he'd had anything to do with dimming the lights in them. "I am serious."

She was clearly skeptical. "You are? You're asking me to marry you?"

He shook his head. "No. I already did that, years ago. The offer still stands."

"It does? I didn't know that." She looked down at the vodka Collins she held and swirled the glass, watching the ice cubes go around in the liquor. A wave of her dark hair fell forward over her shoulder, partially hiding her face from his view.

Kell's heartstrings sang. He could watch her forever. Every movement, every gesture, she made was, to him, liquid poetry. He wanted to build his entire world around her. She was everything to him. He wanted her to be the mother of his children. He wanted to learn about love and friendship from her. Kell had to clear his throat before he could respond. "I didn't know until this moment, either, that my offer still stood, to tell you the truth."

Jamie tugged her hair behind her ear. "Don't tease me like this, Kell. It's not fair."

"Neither is no sex."

"I see. Then you don't agree with me that the sex, which we're very good at and which we substitute for emotional intimacy, is not what is keeping us from having a successful relationship? You don't agree that to give ourselves a fair chance we should abstain and work on a coming together of our minds instead of our bodies?"

Kell could only stare at her. "Baby, you're talking to a man whose profession involves sneaking into hostile territory to spy, then blow up things." When she looked confused, he added, "I'm saying I have no idea what you just said. Can you explain in English, please?"

"Fine. You want to marry me for sex?"

"Sounds good. Yes. I accept."

She smacked his arm.

"Ouch. Come on, honey, marriages have happened with a lot less than that going for them. Hell, Jamie, you and I have been together since we were kids. And there's never been anyone else for either one of us. That has to mean something." Then he eyed the brown bottle, turning it this way and that, reading the label. "But hell, I'd marry you for this beer. I've never seen this brand before. It's great. Where'd you get it?"

"We've gone from marriage to beer." She exhaled

sharply, as if exasperated. "I didn't get it anywhere. It was just in the refrigerator. I guess Greg left it."

Kell's expression hardened. "Who the hell is Greg?"

Jamie shrugged. "Just a guy I dated."

"I guessed that much. You still see him?" He knew it was none of his business—he and Jamie had split up over a year ago—but he couldn't stop himself. "Well?"

Jamie gave him an angry look. "Yes, Kell. I spent all afternoon in bed with you, and now I have a date tonight with Greg. What do you think I am?" She pointed a finger at him. "And you be very careful how you answer that, mister."

Feeling like a lowlife—only now did he realize what he'd accused her of—Kell spread his arms in a gesture of apology. "Hey, I didn't mean anything like that, Jamie, I swear. I was thinking that I haven't been back in your life until the past few days, you could have had an ongoing thing with this Greg guy and just hadn't broken it off yet. That's all."

His words hadn't placated her in the least. That much was evident from the challenging angle of her head. And the sparks of anger lighting her eyes. "That's not what you meant. But from what you just said, can I assume that you're asking me to break off seeing other guys and see you exclusively?"

Kell knew he was losing. He may as well go for broke. "Well, hell yeah, at least by the wedding. I think it's only fair."

That did it. Jamie stood up and stormed away from him, heading for the closed sliding-glass doors that led out onto the balcony. "You're not taking this seriously," she said over her shoulder.

Kell was right behind her. "What makes you say that?" He took her arm and turned her to face him. "Look, I was jealous, okay? I hate the thought of you being with any other guy. Ever. It just kills me inside. I can't help it, and I'm sorry if that makes you mad. But I won't apologize for loving you. And you can just sue me if that's so damn awful."

He glared into her eyes. She glared right back. Tension crackled through the air like electricity. Kell wondered if Jamie was going to have any reaction at all to his saying he loved her. Just as he gave up on eliciting a response, her expression hardened. "You say the word *love*, Kell, but usually only when you're angry or when you're pushed. In those circumstances, it doesn't seem like such a warm emotion. So forgive me if I don't fall at your feet. Besides, I think you have more you want to say. So go ahead, I'm listening."

He'd already had his say, which had ended with the big *L*-word. And she'd pretty much thrown that back in his face. But still, if she wanted to hear more...then, fine. "All right—if you're sure you want to hear this. Because I've got a lot of things I've held inside over the years. But I'm more than willing to share them with you now."

With a belligerent set to her mouth, Jamie said, "Ready when you are."

"Well then, Jamie, have you ever thought about this? All our lives, I've been the one who didn't walk away. I was the one who stayed, the one who was there for you."

"I know that, Kell."

"I don't think you do, Jamie. I think you have me mixed up with your father."

She narrowed her eyes. "Make your point and move on, Kellan David Chance."

He knew this was dangerous ground, but he was determined to have it out with her once and for all. "My point is I'm not your father. I'm not the one who took off on you and your family."

Tears sprang to her eyes. "It was our fault, Kell. Mine and yours. Daddy caught us kissing and then he fought with Mama and left."

She sounded like a little girl. A hurt little girl. "Jamie, you have got to get over that. You're an adult now. Can't you understand what happened? Or are you too close to it? Honey, even I remember your folks fighting long before that day. And more than once. I remember not being more than twelve when you came running to my house with tears streaming down your face because they were having one hell of an argument. Remember? Jamie, it was never going to work between them. You didn't cause him to leave. But I'll tell you this—I'm damn tired of paying for it."

Jamie shook a finger in his face. "Don't you go there, Kell. I *swear* to you, don't...you...go...there."

"I'm already there, Jamie. Because that is exactly what the unspoken thing between us always is. Your father. You don't trust men because of what he did. And I agree, it was pretty awful. I know it was tough because I was there when it happened. And I know it's still hard to face. But you have to, Jamie. You ought to start there for your closure and not hold every other man on the planet accountable for what one man did."

"You don't know what you're talking about." Her hands were fisted, her face was a pale warning for him to stop.

"Like hell I don't. And ever since he left, I've never been able to get 'forever' out of you." He ran a hand through his hair. "Hell, the only way I've been able to breathe so far is by clinging to the hope that the day would come when you'd realize I won't abandon you, that we're supposed to be together for the rest of our lives. But its starting to look like that day will never come."

She stared silently at him. When she finally spoke, her voice was flat. "You're right. It may not."

Challenged, Kell proceeded. "Is that so? Then I have nothing to lose by speaking my mind, do I?"

"You've been doing a fine job of it so far. Don't stop now. This is very enlightening."

"Well, good." Suddenly Kell was beyond angry. He gave in to his passion for her—and his dawning awareness of the futility of it all. "I have allowed you to jerk me around since I was in high school, Jamie, because I love you. But damn, you act as if my loving you is some sort of curse. How many times have I put my life and problems on hold to be at your beck and call?"

"A better question might be how many times have you put your life on the line, Kell. That's always been our biggest problem, the way I see it. Talk about abandonment issues. I'd definitely be alone if you got yourself killed. Do you think maybe that could be a part of my problem with commitment?"

"I might believe it was me and the way I live my life

that was the problem, Jamie...if you'd married some-one else."

That stopped her. She stood there, staring at him, her eyes rounded with what he hoped was a dose of self-realization.

Not that it made him feel any better to win that point. Kell exhaled his frustration. "Look, Jamie, I'm not as good with words and emotions as you are. And I know I'm making a mess of things. But all I can say is I keep trying because I love the hell out of you. And I won't give up until you tell me I don't have a chance. In the meantime, I'll keep going with you to your ther-apist, I'll keep bringing you flowers and stupid cards—"

"I don't think it was stupid."

Could her words indicate a crack in her armor? "You must. It's still over on the table. And it's unopened, as far as I can tell."

"It's not unopened. I read it. It's a beautiful card. And if you'll go check, you'll see the envelope is just turned over the wrong way."

That made him feel a little better. "Well, good. But where are the flowers?" He made a show of looking around the big room. "I don't see them. Did you smell them and throw them away?"

"No. I put them in my office. In a beautiful vase, Kell. You can go check, if you want."

Kell was thoroughly demoralized now. "Jamie, you know what? I can't do this anymore. I'll have a heart attack or something. All I can tell you is I love you, I want to marry you and have babies with you. You know...steps one, two and three. It's that simple to me. But not to you. And I don't know why."

He was finished. His anger, his strength...his hope...drained out of him, leaving him weak. For the longest time, he couldn't seem to look—or walk—away from her. Knowing on some level that he'd gone too far, he shook his head. He hated this moment as much as he loved her. He stalked over to the dining-room table and put the beer bottle on it. "I've got to get out of here," he muttered.

He headed for the front door, each step taking him farther away from where he'd left his heart...with Jamie. But she didn't try to stop him. That was answer enough for him. What a fool he'd been to think she was different now. And what a fool he was for allowing himself to be used again. He jerked the front door open and turned to look at her. She still hadn't moved, but she looked stricken. Still, he couldn't trust the emotion he saw there.

Kell waited. When she still didn't say anything, he exhaled his regret. He'd said too much. All he could do now was make his exit. "You got anything you want to say to me, Jamie, before *I* leave *you* for once?"

"Yes," she said, not sounding at all like herself. "I don't even like Greg."

# 8

THESE THIRTY DAYS were certainly going by fast. Here it was Wednesday...four days after Kell had walked out on her...which meant that almost two weeks had been shaved off the month Dr. Hampton had given her. Jamie stood at Kellan's door, pushing the doorbell button with one hand and, straightening her clothes with the other. She waited. Maybe he wasn't home. Or maybe he could see through the peephole that it was her and he just wouldn't—

The door opened. Jamie's heart gave a leap.

Kell stood there, handsome as ever but straight-faced. For all the warmth he exuded, Jamie figured she might as well have been some door-to-door saleslady with a caseful of makeup. He was dressed in a pair of faded jeans and a powder-blue polo shirt. His shirttail was out, and he was barefoot. Except for one sock. He also needed to shave.

"Are those for me?" he said abruptly.

Feeling suddenly silly, Jamie nevertheless held out to him the hugely expensive bouquet of colorful, exotic flowers she clutched in her fist. "Yes, they are. I thought turnabout would be fair play."

"It is. Thanks." He took them from her, stepped back and closed the door.

Startled, Jamie stared blankly at the white-painted

wooden door. Pursing her lips, she again rang the doorbell.

It opened immediately. Kell still held the flowers. He remained unsmiling. "Yes? Was there something else?"

"Here." She handed him a card. "This is for you, too."

He took the envelope. "Thanks." He stepped back— and again closed the door in her face.

Jamie could *not* believe this. Peeved, she rang the doorbell repeatedly. After a good sustained minute or so of that, it opened again.

Kell stood there...sans flowers and card. "Yes?"

"What do you think you're doing?"

His expression remained impassive as he shrugged. "Answering the door. What are you doing?"

"Getting really tired having it slammed in my face, let me tell you."

"I can imagine. It's not any fun, is it?"

Jamie narrowed her eyes. "What's your point? Is there a lesson in there somewhere?"

Kell's expression indicated he'd thought she'd never ask. "Yes, there is. See, every time I try to be in your life, Jamie—regardless of what I might bring to the relationship—you slam the door in my face. Figuratively speaking, but just as jarring. And I'm about over it. I thought you should know."

His words made her feel foolish and unwanted. With the sweltering heat of the day baking her skin, Jamie just stared at Kell's handsome and, at this moment, harsh face. She knew this man inside and out. Or at least, she thought she did. But maybe she didn't. Because right now he seemed very much a stranger to her.

This called for a shifting of her emotional gears—and a supreme effort not to run away. "Well," she finally said, surprising herself with how strong her voice sounded. "I guess you told me. That was certainly succinct. And psychologically apropos."

"Truth hurts, huh?"

"It stings, actually." She fought to keep her longing for him off her face. It was obvious that Kell was not going to cut her any slack here. Jamie's heart ached. She wanted him so much...the comfort of his arms around her, his love, his respect, his presence in her life. But all she ever did was mess it up for them. She knew she ought to simply say what was in her heart, but she couldn't. There was no need. She'd said it all before—and look how much difference it had made.

"So, Jamie." Kell broke the silence that had grown between them. "Can you tell I've been getting in touch with my feelings by reading this month's edition of *Pop Psychology Today?*"

At least he was still talking to her—and he hadn't slammed the door in her face again. "Sounds like it." Her voice sounded hollow to her ears. "Only I think I'd know if such a magazine existed."

"Well, you got me there. Then would you believe I've been to see Dr. Hampton on my own?"

"No. I was just there yesterday. He would have told me if he'd seen you."

Kell raised his eyebrows. "Oh really? So much for patient confidentiality."

Jamie felt the blush rising in her face. "No, you're

right. He wouldn't have said." She shook her head. "You really didn't see him, did you, Kell? Because that doesn't sound like you."

"In what way?" He looked offended.

Jamie rushed to explain. "It's just that you don't ask for help. You never have."

He stared steadily, soberly, into her eyes. "What makes you think I need help?"

"You do. It's written all over you. Something is bothering you, not that I'm conceited enough to think I'm the cause."

Kell's defensive expression softened. "Nice backtracking. No, I haven't been to see your therapist, Jamie. I don't need a psychiatrist to tell me what I feel in my heart."

"Well, I do. The more I go, the more screwed up I realize I am." Jamie waited, but he didn't say anything. Frustration ate at her. "Kell, this conversation is like being pecked to death by a duck. Don't you want to know what Dr. Hampton and I talked about?"

He shrugged. "Only if you want to tell me." His words were noncommittal, but his dark eyes alertly searched her face.

"I wouldn't be standing here if I didn't want to tell you. Anyway, we..." The words jammed up in her throat. *Courage, Jamie.* She stiffened her resolve to see this through. "We talked about my father. Or my feelings regarding him." Again she waited. He didn't say anything. Jamie exhaled sharply. "Look, I don't deserve a brass band and balloons for that, I know. But I did it for you. Me. Us." When he still he said nothing, she added, "This is where you jump in and say something supportive, Kell."

"Oh." He leaned a shoulder against the doorjamb and crossed his arms over his chest. The coolness radiating from him rivaled the blast of air-conditioned cold that escaped outside as he stood there with the door open. "You didn't need to do it for me, Jamie. You needed to do it for you. Still, I'm glad you talked about your issues regarding your father with your therapist. How'd that go?"

That was an opening…not much of one, but an opening just the same. "It was tough, Kell. Really tough. It hurt a lot." She felt her lips trembling with her unshed tears. "It'll take more than one session, but I think I might be close to accepting the situation as it is now."

"Ah. The elusive closure."

"In a way." Her heart was in her eyes. "Dr. Hampton thought I ought to contact my father and tell him how I feel about what he did. But I can't. I don't know where he is." She wanted to smile, but couldn't.

Kell's eyes thawed a bit. "I'm so sorry, Jamie. That just sucks. I hate that you have to go through this."

She'd thought his coolness was hard. But his sympathy was worse. Dangerously close to tears now, she dragged in a deep breath. "Thank you. I'm glad I went. You're right—it was important. I needed to deal with those feelings."

This was such a stupidly polite conversation. Her heart said *Take me in your arms and hold me. I need you. Help me, Kell.*

But Kell made no move toward her. "Well, I'm glad

you finally did it. But I'm sorry I was such an ass about making you realize that."

His words were apologetic, but his voice remained that of a disinterested stranger. Jamie couldn't seem to get her balance with him. "No need to apologize. But now at least I understand that my father's leaving wasn't my fault. Or yours. I'm sorry I put us through it all these years."

Kell nodded and almost smiled. "Don't be. It's okay. So, what are you doing here?"

She exhaled. "I'm trying to apologize, to say you were right and I was wrong. I'm glad you were the one to walk away because now I don't have to worry about how I'd feel if you did. Ta-da. The world didn't end, and you're still talking to me." She sobered. "And I really don't like Greg."

Kell shook his head. "Greg again. I still don't know what that means."

"It means our fuss began over his stupid beer."

"No, it didn't."

"Yes, it did. In a way. But, anyway, am I forgiven?"

"Is that why you're here...forgiveness? Okay. But for what exactly? I want to be sure we're on the same page."

Feeling better by the minute—they were honestly communicating now—Jamie playfully pursed her lips. "Do I have to eat my humble pie out here, Kell? As hot as it is, it's bound to burn before I can get it all down."

He chuckled and waved her inside. "Come on in. It's cheaper to let you inside than it would be to stand there with the door open and continue to air-condition my front porch."

Jamie stepped inside and felt the blessed coolness of the inside air on her skin. She turned and Kell's gaze met hers. The naked look of uncertainty in his eyes surprised Jamie. Somehow, seeing that, she felt even better. He did care. She attempted a smile. "This isn't going at all how I'd envisioned."

"Really? What did you see happening? Some big soap opera-worthy 'reunited' scene with violin music playing in the background?"

Jamie just grinned. "You've been home alone too long, Kell. You have got to stop watching daytime TV." She plopped her purse on the dining-room table and met his gaze. "It's good to see you again. I've missed you. I probably don't have any right to say that, but I did."

He ran a hand through his hair. "You have every right," he said softly.

Filled with yearning for his touch, which he still denied her, she roved her gaze over him, loving everything about his appearance. The man could fill out a pair of jeans. And what his muscled physique did for that knit shirt should be illegal. She looked down his length. He had on only one sock. Suddenly Jamie felt terrible for ogling him because that one sock made him seem so vulnerable, like a little boy.

As always, his vulnerability frightened her. She covered it by indicating his appearance. "Were you just leaving or just getting home? I can't tell."

"Getting ready to go out. Jeff had some complications that required more surgery. I was on my way to the hospital to see him."

Fear shot through Jamie. She didn't know Jeff, but

she'd met Melanie, and she knew that somehow Kell's emotional state was tied up in Jeff's condition. "Oh, I'm so sorry to hear that. Look, I can just leave." She picked up her purse and turned toward the door. "I hope he's okay. Please tell his wife—"

"Jamie, wait. Please."

She pivoted to face him. His expression was troubled. Her heart pounding, Jamie took a step toward him. "Kell? Are you all right?"

He held a hand up to stop her. His throat worked and he blinked. Then once he got himself under control again, he asked, "Will you go with me to see him?"

Warmth spread through Jamie. He needed her. Jamie nodded and again put her purse down. "I'd be honored. And I'm sorry—sincerely sorry, Kell—that I came over here with the flowers and a card at a time like this."

"It's okay. They're nice. I've never been given flowers before." He didn't say anything else. He looked around the small dining room as if he'd forgotten what he'd been about to do.

Before the ensuing silence could become uncomfortable, Jamie leaped into action, heading for his small kitchen. "Hey, I'll just go put the flowers in some water while you finish getting dressed. Do you have a vase?"

"No. Just use whatever you can find. It doesn't matter. Nothing in my kitchen is sacred."

Jamie turned to face him. He again looked so much like a hurt child that her heart went out to him. Once more she felt unsure that she should be here. "Look, Kell, you've got a lot on your plate right now. Why don't I just go? I don't really need to be here adding to your stress load with my problems. Somehow, in the face of what you seem to be going through—I have to say 'seem' because you won't tell me what it is—my difficulties getting my license to practice seem trivial and so self-centered."

"No, they're not. Not to me." His tone was adamant. "Nothing to do with you has ever been trivial, Jamie. Whether it was teaching you how to throw a baseball or taking you to the senior prom. You should know that by now."

She smiled, but she was on a roll now. "Well, that's nice of you to say. But maybe right now isn't the best time for me and you to try to...do whatever it is we're trying to do here."

"Wrong. You're not going to walk out on me. Not now. Not ever again. Look, it's not easy for me to say these things...but I'd like you to stay. Just be with me, okay?"

His words thrilled Jamie's heart. "Okay," she said quietly. "Why don't I just—" She gestured vaguely toward the kitchen. "Take care of the flowers and then we'll go. I can drive, if you like."

He shook his head. "No. We'll take my car since it has a base sticker."

"Oh. I hadn't thought about that. Your friend's in the hospital at MacDill." She wanted so much to take Kell in her arms and hold him and tell him that everything would be okay. But she didn't know if he would want her to do that...and she really wasn't sure that everything would be okay. With Jeff. Or with her and Kell.

Lost in her uncertainty, Jamie stood where she was and watched Kell walk by her. He didn't pause to touch her or say anything. She ached with wanting to reach out and feel him but she didn't dare. So she stood there, with her heart dragging, watching him sprint up the stairs—and marveled at how that nasty sutured wound on his thigh never seemed to bother him. She felt certain that if he ever chose to tell her how it had happened, then she and he would be okay together. It would mean he trusted her with that side of his life.

Jamie turned away from the stairs, and went into the kitchen. She wished Kell would realize that she wanted to know about every part of his life, his work included. Yeah, right. Like she hadn't railed at him about his risky job every time he tried to tell her something. Jamie sighed. She was the problem, not Kell. If anyone had some changing to do, it was her. She needed to work on her responses to his risk-taking. That, after all, was all she could control.

While she searched her psychologist's repertoire for strategies to get Kell to open up to her, Jamie searched his kitchen cabinets for something suitable to put the flowers in. Suddenly she realized she was wondering how Melanie handled her fears for her husband. Weren't they the same as hers for Kell? Jamie smiled to herself. Of course. She could talk to Melanie. What an obvious answer! And just as suddenly, she noticed a tall ceramic beer stein. It was perfect for the flowers. Jamie pulled it down, ran some water into it, and then reached for the flowers, which Kell had placed on the countertop beside the stove.

Jamie picked them up and began unwrapping them. At least he hadn't flung them in the garbage can as he'd accused her of doing with the ones he'd brought her.

Jamie sighed, seeing in her mind's eye the beautiful arrangement sitting in a crystal vase on her desk. His opened card sat beside them. He'd been unfair to accuse her of throwing them away. But still, she supposed she deserved Kell's defensiveness. In fact, after his tirade the other evening, she'd done a lot of thinking about what he'd said.

Jamie rested the heels of her hands against the counter and stared into the dining room. But all she could see was the vicious circle that represented their past together. His daredevil ways set off her fear of abandonment. His trying to change for her made him miserable and resentful. Then she'd tell him to—literally—go jump off a cliff. He would. Then she got even more scared.

She needed to change that. Giving herself an emotional shake, Jamie adjusted a bit of greenery in the arrangement.

"You done here? The flowers look great."

Jamie jumped, putting a hand to her throat. "I didn't even hear you come down the stairs. You startled me."

"Yeah, I noticed that. Sorry. Habit and training. But what were you thinking so deeply about? I've been standing here a good thirty seconds. I even said your name once."

Her face heated up. "You did? Wow."

"Yeah. Where'd you go?"

Jamie didn't speak right away. Instead, she took in his appearance, as if she needed to verify for herself whom she was addressing. He looked the same as he had earlier, only neater. His shirt was tucked in. He had on shoes and socks. He'd shaved. In his hands were a pair of dark aviator sunglasses and a set of car keys. Gone was the uncertain little boy of a few minutes ago. Here was the confident, sexy man awaiting her answer.

"Where'd I go?" she said, meeting his gaze...and finding she was reluctant to tell him just yet. "A foreign place, actually."

He grinned. "I've been there. I like the people, but the weather leaves something to be desired. And for what it's worth, don't drink the water."

Jamie smiled weakly. *Something to be desired*, he'd said. She believed she now knew what that something was. Emotional intimacy. If they could achieve it, that would be one kind of closure. If they didn't...well, that would be another kind. A bad kind. A final kind.

"So, are you done here? Visiting hours aren't all that long."

Close to tears because she didn't know which outcome they'd have, Jamie grabbed the stein and swept by Kell, putting the flowers on the dining-room table.

"Hey, those look great in there," he said. "Thank you, Jamie."

Jamie preened under his appreciation. "You're welcome. I'll just go get my purse."

But when she turned around, Kell was right behind her. He took her in his arms and hugged her to him. Jamie melted against him, loving the citrusy scent of his after-shave and the warm feel of his body pressed against hers. But most of all she reveled in how her body contoured itself to his...as if only when they were together were they one. Kell kissed the top of her head.

Jamie pulled back in his embrace and managed to smile up at him. "I'm glad you asked me to stay, Kell."

"Me, too," he said. "And I'm glad that you didn't walk away. This feels like a beginning, Jamie, when before all I could see were endings."

# 9

JAMIE WISHED that she hadn't come with Kell. They were in Jeff Camden's hospital room and she felt like a complete outsider. She'd forgotten he and his wife and Kell were such close friends. The situation was awkward at best—much as if she'd wandered into a stranger's room and didn't know how to get out. After all, she didn't know the man in the bed. And he didn't know her. So after the initial introduction, what could he say to her? *Shrunk any heads lately?* Or her to him. *Hey, what's that tube connected to?* Hardly.

The poor guy had to feel pretty helpless lying there with those tubes running in and out of him. And Melanie was understandably fussing over her husband and adding only peripherally to the spatter of conversation. Kell, too, seemed to have trouble making conversation, trying his best to be upbeat and not talk about anything in particular. Sports. Weather. Cars. Sports. No one had to tell Jamie that if she and Melanie hadn't been in the room, the subject of women would have been liberally peppered throughout their conversation, too.

Jamie was seeing a new side of Kell, a side she was proud of. Talking about normal everyday guy stuff would make Jeff feel like part of the world again. And Jamie couldn't help enjoying the interaction between the two men. It helped her focus outside herself. As always, if Kell was anywhere around, she watched him. She's seen him all his life with his brothers, but now he was with a peer, one he had met sometime after she and he had parted ways a year ago. But it was obvious they'd quickly become close. Sharing life-threatening experiences had a way of hastening the process. There was ample data to support that phenomenon. And now she was seeing it in action.

She was also having a struggle with the green-eyed monster of jealousy. Melanie Camden and Kell related to each other well...too well. She knew there was nothing sexual about it. And Jamie's jealousy wasn't even based on the fact that Melanie was beautiful and smart, warm or charming. And she was all of those things, Jamie grumbled, giving the woman her due.

No, what Jamie was jealous of was that the other woman had Kell's ear. Jamie knew he had talked to Melanie about things he hadn't felt he could talk about with her. It wasn't fair. Or right. Melanie even knew that she and Kell were physically intimate. She also knew what had happened to land her husband in his present dire straits. And more importantly, she knew how Kell had been injured. She just knew everything...and Jamie knew nothing. And the three of them—Kell, Jeff and Melanie—were having a reunion, leaving Jamie to stand to one side, her smile painted on, trying to look as if she knew what everyone was talking about. When she didn't.

A few minutes later, wouldn't you know it, Melanie noticed Jamie's awkwardness. *Great—she's also kind and sensitive. Let me slit my wrists.* The other woman had taken one look at Jamie and had announced that the two men could talk, and that she and Jamie would leave them alone for the moment. Jamie had followed her out, intending to make it a point to ask Melanie some questions about how she handled the dangerous side of her husband's career.

So there they were, huddled in the doorway of the hospital room.

"He looks terrible, doesn't he?"

Melanie's whispered question had Jamie glancing toward the two men. As always, her gaze lit first on Kell, but she focused now on Jeff Camden, noting his pale, haggard appearance. She turned to the worried woman at her side. Melanie's expression was pinched, and she was hugging herself. Gone was the jealousy Jamie had been feeling toward this woman.

Keeping her voice soothing, Jamie heard herself say, "Well, he's been through a lot, Melanie. He's bound to look a bit rough around the edges."

*What a brilliant observation*, Jamie chastised herself. How lame.

But Melanie didn't seem to notice. "I know," she said, nodding. "He's so pale and thin now. Honey, I wish you could have seen him before. Whew. So tan and robust." She turned a brave smile Jamie's way. "I just hate this, but at least he's alive and is going to be okay."

"That's the important thing." Again, Jamie heard her own words and frowned...when had she developed this milk-toast bedside manner? She was supposed to be the hip guru to the young crowd. And here she sounded like her great-grandma. Well, at least her words seemed to be striking all the right chords with Melanie.

"You're right, of course. And I'm very grateful for his well-being." Melanie gestured toward the men. "Look at Kell, will you? I swear, he's about one night's lost sleep away from being in that empty bed next to Jeff's."

Though her conscience pricked her, Jamie tried not to feel as if the stress on Kell's face was her fault.

Melanie kept talking. "He needs to quit blaming himself for what happened. It wasn't his fault. We've all told him that. But will he listen? No."

Even though she was dying to ask for details, Jamie didn't feel she could. Nor did she want to admit that Kell hadn't told her anything. So she simply said, "Sounds like the Kell I know."

Melanie smiled at her. "And you do know him better than anyone, don't you?"

The question made Jamie's heart hurt. She couldn't quite hold Melanie's steady gaze. "I used to, Melanie. But I don't anymore. I think you probably know him better than I do now."

Melanie frowned. "Why do you say that?"

"Because you're his friend. He talks to you."

"He does." Melanie's smile warmed. "But about you. Always about you."

She said it in such an intimate way that Jamie felt her face color. "Well, I guess I have no secrets left, do I?"

Melanie laughed. "You have plenty of secrets, Jamie. But speaking of Kell, I'm hoping Jeff's being home will help him come to grips with everything. I swear, Kell wears his command on his sleeve like most people do their hearts. But there's something outside the job that's bothering him. I can't quite put my finger on it. But he looks more stressed than usual, even for him. What else do you suppose is wrong?"

The question was a pointed one, and not lost on Jamie. Melanie knew—and she was fishing. Jamie shrugged, choosing to remain purposely obtuse. "I don't know."

Melanie let out a sigh and shook her head. "I am so sorry, Jamie. I was being nosy, wasn't I? My manners are usually better than this. It's none of my business what's going on between you two, is it?"

*No* was the simple answer. But Melanie was so disarmingly apologetic. And Jamie still had the desire to pick this woman's brain regarding ways of coming to grips with the risky careers of the men they loved. So she smiled. "Don't worry about it, Melanie. It's not as if Kell doesn't keep making it your business, anyway." Now, that didn't sound right. "I mean it's okay. Really."

Melanie looked contrite. "You're upset because he talks to me, aren't you?" She touched Jamie's arm. "Please don't be. I like Kell tremendously. He's been through a lot, and it's just natural that he'd want to talk about it. In a way, I went through their ordeal with them. It's nothing more than that."

How nice could one woman get? Jamie shook her head. "Don't sell yourself short, Melanie. I think it's a lot more than that. And who better than me, a psychologist, to have some understanding of the effect a common crisis can have on its participants?" Jamie heard her own words—clinical, textbook. "And no, I don't always talk like that," she added wryly.

She punctuated her words with a smile. It suddenly seemed important to her that she impress Melanie. Probably so the Atlanta beauty could report to Kell that she too liked Jamie. Since they were friends, Kell and Melanie, Jamie wanted to be her friend, too.

Melanie returned Jamie's smile. "You're so kind, Jamie. I really do like you. And it's not like I don't know for myself what's stuck in Kell's craw." Her expression became sober. "It was that damn mission. Everyone says it failed. Well, it didn't. They accomplished their objective—hit their target, I mean—but men were wounded. And keeping their men safe is a source of pride with the SEALs. But accidents happen. It certainly wasn't Kell's fault. We've all been trying to convince him of that, but he won't hear it. Silly male pride. Anyway, they got bad intel and everyone knows it. That's what almost got Jeff and Kell killed."

Fear shot through Jamie, weakening her knees. Kell had almost been killed. Apparently that healing gash on his right thigh didn't tell the whole story. This was her worst nightmare come to life. Still, she needed to get the terms right. "They got bad what, Melanie? 'Intel,' did you say?"

Melanie nodded. "Yes. You know…intelligence… before their mission. And getting that wrong is not tolerated, honey. Believe me, heads have already rolled at the base."

Melanie's words nearly stopped Jamie's heart. She hated Kell's daredevil profession but worried now about his emotional well-being because she knew *he* loved it, had devoted himself to it, and defined himself by it. "Oh, God, Melanie, is Kell's head one of the ones that rolled? Is that what's wrong with him? He acted like it was the end of the world when he told me he has a desk job now."

"He would think that. But, yes, in a way, Jamie, he was reprimanded. He's getting a promotion to full commander out of this, but that doesn't help. I guess it's sent him a mixed message…'Your mission ended badly through no fault of your own, so we're going to relieve you of command out in the field but give you a promotion and a nice safe desk job in the States.' I swear. I believe that right now Kell thinks his career is over. But I don't think that's true."

Jamie made a scoffing sound. "Try to get him to believe that."

"I have tried. But to no avail. You see, when their team went over to Europe to Chech—"

"Melanie," Jamie said. She looked up and down the hallway behind them. "Should we really be talking about this? I mean, Kell hasn't said anything at all to me about what happened. And we are on a military base. I'd hate to be hauled away, never to be seen again."

Melanie chuckled. "Oh, it's okay. There're no secrets from us. We wives eventually learn all about what's going on with our men."

Jamie looked down. "You forget, Melanie…I'm not one of the wives."

"Well, you will be, if you're smart."

Jamie snapped her head up. "If I'm smart?" She had

her *I don't need a man to complete me* speech ready to go, but Melanie spoke first.

"That's right. If you're smart. And I think you are." Melanie's finely arched eyebrows lowered. "Look, honey, don't let this Southern-belle exterior fool you. I'm a modern woman, too, just like you. I have a career as a freelance writer. I work from home, and I'm all about equal pay and respect. But I'm not talking about the workplace now, or society's perceptions of how any woman should live her life. What I'm talking about are affairs of the heart, something strictly personal. Jamie, Kell loves you. Now, I don't know how you feel about him, but because he's my friend, I'm just going to come right out with it. I think it's you who's killing him."

Melanie's words were like a slap in the face. And a wake-up call. Jamie slumped. "Oh, Melanie. What am I going to do? I just don't know how to get through to him—"

"Shh." Melanie put a hand on Jamie's arm and turned her away from the men behind them. "Hold that thought for just a minute." She looked over her shoulder to the scene behind them.

Jamie followed her direction, seeing Kell and Jeff talking quietly. They were paying no attention to the two women huddled in the room's doorway. "Is something wrong?" she asked.

"Everything is fine," Melanie answered. "I just want to talk to you in private. I think the cafeteria is open downstairs." She called out over her shoulder, "We'll be right back, y'all. We're going to visit the ladies' room. Don't you go anywhere, you hear?"

The men looked their way. Kell spoke for them. "We won't." His gaze lit on Jamie, skewering her in place. "Whatever Melanie says to you about me, it's not true."

"Kellan Chance, are you calling me a liar?" Melanie challenged.

"Oh, so you *are* going to talk about me."

Melanie pursed her lips. "Smart-aleck man. You wish." She blew her husband a kiss and then dragged Jamie out of the room with her.

KELL TURNED his attention back to Jeff. "Oh, man, the two of them together can't be good."

A thin smile split Jeff's pale face. "You're a cooked goose, buddy."

Jeff's voice was hoarse, barely loud enough to be heard. Kell's heart thudded heavily, guiltily. This man—his best friend in the world after his two brothers—was in this condition...because of Kell's failed leadership.

"Let it go. It's not...your fault, man," Jeff said with some effort.

Meeting his friend's sincere gaze, Kell realized his own expression must have given away his thoughts. "You and everyone else keep saying that, Jeff. So who're *you* trying to convince—me or you?"

Jeff slowly raised a finger and pointed it Kell's way. "You."

"You can't do it, buddy. Bottom-line responsibility is mine. I know it, and you know it."

Jeff wet his lips and took a breath...a painful breath

as evidenced by his grimace. "Don't...eat yourself up, Kell. I...knew the risk. And I'm fine."

Kell grunted his disagreement. "Yeah, you look fine. Like some damn refugee from a POW camp."

Jeff managed a shaky grin. "I'd do...anything...to get out of...mowing the lawn."

"I hear you, slacker." This banter reassured Kell that Jeff was intact mentally if not yet physically. Still, Kell hurt just to look at his friend. Before the mission a little over two weeks ago, Jeff had been vigorous, full of laughter, and with a healthy life ahead of him. Now look at him. But the good news was that the man had come home to a beautiful wife who loved him. And he still had a successful military career in the making— and every reason to live. Kell tried to focus on that, but suddenly it all got to him. "Jeff, I—hell, man, I'd trade places with you in a heartbeat, if I could."

"You...almost did," Jeff reminded him.

It was a painful truth. Jeff had saved his life. "I know. And you damn near got yourself killed for your heroics. I still owe you a butt-kicking for that when you're on your feet again."

Jeff grinned and, for a second, looked like his old self. "Something to...look forward to." He then pointed to a plastic water pitcher and a cup on the bedside tray just out of his reach. "Can you...get that for me?"

Kell jumped up. Activity was good. He wasn't much for conversation. How many times could he say he was sorry? "Sure. No problem, man."

He poured the water and turned to Jeff, staring at him. Seeing his friend's hollow features ate at Kell's gut. His hand tightened around the cup. He wanted to throw it against the wall and rage against the injustice of it all. The anger, the helplessness…he and his men were supposed to be invincible. Kell inhaled deeply and collected himself. "Can you do this by yourself? Do I need to—"

"I can do it." Jeff's sharp words exposed a world of pride and stubbornness underneath. That was good. An attitude like that would get him through the tough times ahead.

"Here you go." Kell handed the cup to Jeff, thankful that at least he could drink unaided. As he watched Jeff's precise yet unsteady movements…reminiscent of an old man's…Kell had to swallow and grit his teeth together. "So, what happened to put you back in the hospital?"

He took the cup from Jeff, placed it back on the tray and sat down.

Jeff shrugged, grimaced. "Last night. Pain. Internal bleeding. Something not sutured right. Surgeons fixed it."

"Hell." Kell sat forward in his chair and rubbed his hands over his face. Then he looked into Jeff's kind, hazel eyes. "Man, this sucks. I'd give anything if I was in that bed instead of you."

Jeff shook his head. "You wouldn't like it."

"I don't like it now."

Jeff stared at him a moment. "I'm going…to be fine, Kell. I need…you to believe that, too."

"I will when you stop looking like death warmed over."

Jeff raised his eyebrows. "Thanks. I love you, too."

Pretending shock, Kell sat up, looking around as if making sure they were alone. "Don't let that get around. I'd like to preserve what's left of my career, if you don't mind."

Jeff's eyes lit with humor but then he sobered. "Melanie told me." He took a few more breaths. "Congratulations, Commander."

Kell sent him a mock salute. "At ease, Lieutenant Camden." Then he downplayed his promotion. "It comes with a desk job. I can hardly wait."

"You're going to be a paper pusher?"

"Yeah. In fact, I'm thinking of recommending you to be on my staff just so you can't laugh at me."

Jeff's gaze was unwavering. "I'd be honored."

That got to Kell. He couldn't speak. He suddenly realized that he'd only been half teasing when he'd offered the job to Jeff. "You would? You'd put your life in my hands again?"

"In a heartbeat."

Kell couldn't look away from the look of respect that radiated from his friend's eyes. Overcome with emotion, his mouth working, his eyes burning, Kell came to his feet and stalked over to the window, staring out at the parking lot. He cleared his throat. "You don't have to say that, Jeff."

"I know. But since we'd...be inside a building...I figure the worst you could do was...trip me going down the stairs."

Kell let out a burst of laughter. With the macho equilibrium restored between them, he turned around and walked back to his friend's bedside. "And I just might do that, too, you son of a gun. Are you serious, though? Would you consider coming in from the field?"

Jeff nodded. His expression warmed. He licked at his lips. "Melanie just told me...she's pregnant, Kell. Just found out today."

Happiness tore through Kell. "Oh, hell, Jeff. That's great news, man."

Jeff nodded, seemed to start mending right before Kell's eyes. "Five years we've been trying, Kell. Five years."

Kell gave Jeff a gentle high-five. "I can't believe it. This is fabulous news. You've got to be so happy."

Jeff nodded. "We are. Thrilled. We want you...to be the...godfather."

As if someone had pushed him, Kell sat down heavily in the chair behind him. "Whoa. Me a godfather? You sure?"

"Can't think of...anyone better, Kell."

Kell smiled, feeling happy all the way through. He placed his fist over his heart. "You honor me, my friend."

Jeff nodded, then his eyes became pleading. "I can't...do this anymore, Kell. Playing the warrior. It's...too hard on Melanie. She doesn't...say anything, but she worries. And now she's expecting. I'd just appreciate it if...there's anything you can do to...get me in out of the field."

Kell sat forward in his chair, energized by this opportunity to do something positive for his friend. "I'll move heaven and earth if I have to, Jeff. I swear it to you. It will happen."

"What about...you and Jamie? She's great. Beautiful."

Grinning, Kell shook his head. "She's all that and more. Smart. Funny. Too smart for me. But who knows, Jeff? I sure as hell don't. We can't ever seem to get it together. She hates my career, but unlike Melanie, she doesn't keep her thoughts to herself."

"Melanie worries. It's only natural...when you care."

"Yeah, you're right. But Jamie takes it a step further. She retreats, cuts me out of her life. Every time we get close, something happens and she drops me cold."

"That's tough, man. You love her, don't you?"

"Yeah. So what's your secret? How do you and Melanie make it work, Jeff?"

"We talk. I let her in...my head, my heart. Don't hold back."

Kell frowned. "I don't know if I can do that."

"You have to. It's...the only way."

Kell rubbed his aching thigh and shook his head. For perhaps the first time, he was seeing directly how his career affected every aspect of his life. It was like seeing Jeff, all beat to hell and in a hospital bed, and noticing Melanie's worry, brought it all home. Kell finally understood that he couldn't put his job in one box and Jamie in another. Maybe the two needed to be in the same box. And maybe, instead of brushing aside her fears for him, instead of telling her his job had nothing to do with her, he needed to include her. Wasn't that what Jeff had said?

"How's your leg?"

Kell looked up and realized he was still rubbing his

leg. "Okay. The sutures come out tomorrow. It aches, but it doesn't bother me as much as trying to figure out this thing with Jamie."

Jeff grinned. "Never knew you...to have...problems with women."

Kell chuckled. "That's because I didn't really love any of them. None of them got to me, you know what I mean?"

Jeff nodded. "I do. Melanie got to me."

"That's a no-brainer, buddy. Melanie gets to everybody." Kell frowned and glanced toward the open doorway to the hall. "And right now, she's probably getting to Jamie with stories about me."

"Start worrying, my friend."

Kell again focused on Jeff. "I already have. About a lot of things."

Jeff shifted a bit in his bed as if trying to get more comfortable. "Like what?"

"Like thinking you're right about a desk job. I'm not as upset about it as I thought I'd be."

Jeff nodded. "And you don't have to be...alone anymore, either, Kell."

Kell grinned, defensively. "Did you take a knock on the head over there that I don't know about? Something that pounded some smarts into you?"

"No. I just...came home to what matters."

Kell met his friend's all-too-knowing eyes. Kell knew what really mattered to him. Jamie. He could hear her voice, her laughter, could feel her touch on his skin...her kiss on his mouth. His career would end one day, but he would always love Jamie. Shouldn't that tell him something?

"Need to...make that woman yours, Kell." Jeff's words sliced through the silence in the room.

"I keep trying, man. But she keeps running."

Jeff nodded. "Kell, I want you to...do something...for me, okay?"

"Sure." Kell jumped at the chance, knowing there was nothing he could deny Jeff. "Just tell me what it is. Whatever you want."

"Ask Jamie to marry you."

# 10

TWO NIGHTS LATER, their first chance to be together and talk, Jamie and Kell were walking along Indian Rocks Beach. Night had settled around them like a warm and familiar blanket. The moon was full, its silver-gray light illuminating the restless water and their shadowed figures. Overhead, stars winked. Offshore, the lights on numerous anchored yachts seemed also to be a part of the sky.

The breaking surf provided a serenade for their moonlight stroll. She and Kell. Two lovers, hand in hand. A soft sea breeze blew and gently lifted Jamie's hair and her long ivory skirt. Her sandals dangled from her fingers by their narrow leather straps. Kell had his pant legs rolled up a few turns and carried his shoes in one hand, too. To their right, unceasing waves, caressed the sandy shore.

This was the height of romance. Jamie smiled contentedly and breathed in deeply of the salty air.

Kell suddenly stopped and pulled her against his warm body, eliciting a surprised yelp from her. Two pairs of shoes tumbled to the sand. "Marry me, Jamie. Right now. Tonight. Don't think about it. Just marry me."

Struck speechless, she stared at him. "Have you lost

your mind?" She pressed her hand to his forehead. "Well, you feel cool. But I think you're feverish."

"Yes, I am feverish. For you." He captured her hand, kissing her palm, teasing her sensitive skin with his teeth. A jet of desire rocketed through Jamie. In the moonlight, his dark eyes sparkled with ardor. "And I'm completely serious," he said, his voice husky. "Marry me, Jamie."

Everything inside her screamed for her to say yes. But her practical adult side urged on her the caution born of their two past and failed attempts at being a couple. Which left Jamie not knowing what to say. She was saved for a few wit-gathering moments by another couple who strolled slowly by them and spoke in passing. When the couple was a distance away, out of earshot, Jamie spoke. "I want to—very much, Kell. But not like this."

"Why not?" He held her tighter in his arms and trailed slow, sensual kisses from her collarbone to her earlobe.

Jamie's eyes fluttered closed as she melted against Kell. Clinging to his broad, muscled shoulders, she heard her breath coming in short gasps. "Stop that. It's not fair. I can't think with you pressed this close to me, doing the things you're doing to me."

He lifted his head and looked deeply into her eyes. "But I like doing these things to you, Jamie. And I like it even better being pressed up against you like this."

Grinning, Jamie boldly rubbed her self against him. "I can tell, Commander Chance. I'm impressed."

Kell's husky chuckle sent a delicious shiver down

her spine. "As you can feel, I want to make love to you here on this beach. Right now."

"My, my, you are impetuous tonight. First you want to marry me and then you want to make love to me, all in the same night."

Kell pulled back. The bright moonlight illuminated the look of bemusement on his face. "Well, that's the right sequence, isn't it? First comes love, then comes marriage, then comes making love on a moonlit beach."

Jamie pretended to think about it. "No. I think that's wrong. I think next is a baby carriage."

"Not without the making-love part first."

"That's true."

"So you'll marry me?"

Again, Jamie stalled. "If it was that easy, Kell, we'd already be married." Reality settled in over her. "And divorced, too, I'd bet," she added in a low voice.

Kell frowned. "I don't like the sound of that. You don't think we could've kept it all together?"

Jamie lowered her gaze. Staring at his shirt button, she fiddled with it as she spoke. "No, I don't. Not the way we used to be when we were together, Kell."

"I see. But what about now? You don't think we've changed, maybe learned a few things, in the last year?"

Jamie shrugged. "I don't know. Maybe. But we've just reconnected, so it's hard to say. All I know is we never could make it last. But what's really different now?"

"A hell of a lot is different, Jamie. We talk more now. I've got a desk job, which means I'll be around. And you're out of school. You've got your future ahead of you. The way I see it, the only thing that hasn't changed is how much I love you. I always have. And I always will."

His words thrilled her as much as his touch did. Jamie smiled up at him and put her fingertips to his warm, firm lips. "I will always love you, too."

His grip tightened momentarily. "I don't think I like the way you said that, Jamie. It sounded like there was a 'but' that should have followed it. Instead of a happily ever after."

Jamie pulled back a bit. "We're talking fairy tales now? I don't believe in them, Kell. My mother thought she had happily ever after and look what happened? And you know what? It doesn't change anything for her. She still loves my father. And he's a man who just up and left us one day."

Kell's body went rigid. "There it is. Your father again."

Fearing he was about to release her, Jamie tightly held on to Kell, wadding his crisp cotton shirt in her fists. "No, hear me out. I'm not comparing you to my father. I know you're not him. And there is no 'but.' I'm just using my parents as one example for caution here."

"And a bad example, too, Jamie. You're looking for guarantees. But there aren't any. Not in any part of life. But if you want examples, my parents have been married over thirty-five years, and they're still going strong. Lots of couples make it."

"I know that. I've done the research."

"Then you know I don't have ironclad guarantees to give you. But I am willing to sign my name on the dotted line of a marriage certificate with you, Jamie. And I've never met another woman I'd say those words to. It's always only been you for me. That has to mean something, dammit."

"It does, Kell. It means everything to me." Jamie abandoned her resistance and rested her forehead against his shoulder. With every breath she took, she inhaled the clean, masculine scent of him...such a heady aphrodisiac. "Oh, Kell. I love you so much."

"So...is that a yes?"

She chuckled softly. "You are relentless." She looked up at him, loving the firm sensuality of his mouth, the dark fires smoldering in his eyes. "No, it isn't—not for tonight and not like this. For one thing, it's almost midnight. Where would we go to get married?"

"Las Vegas."

"Las Vegas?" She pulled back in his arms. "You've given this some thought, haven't you?"

"I have."

"But it's so sudden."

"No, it isn't."

Jamie could only stare blankly at him. "We don't even have a marriage license."

"Okay, is *that* a yes?"

She bit at her bottom lip. "I'm not sure."

"Aha. Then there's hope. We can get a license in Nevada. Handing those things out is one of their major industries."

She searched his face. "You're serious, aren't you?"

"As a heart attack."

"Kell, we can't do this. We don't even have luggage

or airplane tickets. I'm not even sure there are flights out at this time of night."

He kissed the tip of her nose. "Quit being so damn practical, will you? Haven't you ever wished we could just run off together?"

"But we have to—"

"Jamie, do you love me? I mean really. Passionately."

A warm thrill washed over her skin. "More than anything. You have to know that. And that's why I'm hesitating—*because* I want this to work, Kell. I *want* us to have forever. You're my only chance at happiness. And that's what scares me."

"I don't get it. If I'm your only chance at happiness, then—"

"What if I make a commitment...and it doesn't work out? Well, then, I'll never have any happiness. This way at least I have some hope. Does that make sense?"

"Hell no. So, let's go. Right now." He took her hand and started hauling her across the sand.

After several bounding steps, Jamie dug her heels in and tugged on his hand, which was clasped around her wrist. "Stop."

He turned to her. "Yes?"

She pointed back the way they'd come. "We left our shoes back there, Kell. They're going to get washed away."

He frowned and stared toward the water...and then shrugged his shoulders. "The hell with them. We have other shoes. I'll buy you new ones in Las Vegas. Some really glitzy ones with high heels and sequins. Red ones."

"I don't think so." Jamie shook her head, chuckling. "You are absolutely insane. You expect us to get on a plane, barefoot and sandy, then fly to Las Vegas without luggage and get married? And then we can fly back here and make love on the beach?"

"I like the way you think."

"Stop it, Kell. You're scaring me. I need time to think."

"You can think on the way to the airport."

"No, I can't. Seriously, I don't want to rush into this and make a mistake we'll both end up regretting."

He heaved a dramatic sigh. "All right. Fine." He released her arm and plopped down in the sand, sitting with his knees bent and his arms resting atop them. "Take your time. But this is the last time I'm offering. After this, if it's a no-go, then I'm withdrawing my offer."

Jamie froze, too scared even to contemplate such a thing. "Don't say that. Please."

"You know, that's all you keep saying to me. 'No.' Well, now I'm listening to you."

She tipped her chin up. "I haven't said no."

He tossed a handful of sand at her feet. "Then are you saying yes?"

She shook her feet, ridding them of the sand. "No."

"Why not?"

"Because it's just occurred to me what this is. And I don't even think you're aware of it."

"Okay, I'll bite. What is this that I'm not aware of?"

"This, for you, is the same thrill you'd get jumping out of an airplane. Or off a cliff. Or into enemy territory. Anything to get the adrenaline pumping. You've always been an adrenaline junkie, Kell. A thrill seeker—"

"Wait." He held his hand up. "I've already heard this speech."

He sounded disgusted, but Jamie couldn't help herself. This was too important. "I know you have. And I hate to nag you, but the truth is...you've lived this speech. We both have. And I'm afraid that's what a spur-of-the-moment wedding would be for you—the next thrill. What comes after that? The letdown? The boredom? That's what I'm afraid of. You'd get that 'been there, done that' feeling and then off you'd go, seeking excitement. Without me."

Kell hung his head and slowly shook it. Jamie feared she'd gone too far. But there was nothing she could do now but wait.

After a quiet moment he looked up at her. "I don't think I deserve that, Jamie. The only times I've ever been without you were when you left. Not the other way around. All I can say is there's no risk here. I never want to be without you. And you don't have to worry—I'm not a thrill seeker. Not anymore."

"Oh, Kell, come on. It can't be that easy."

"I'm telling you it is. I've changed."

"Have you really? See, I think that whatever happened to you and Jeff has you off-kilter right now. But that's all. I think you'll get over it...and want to go right back to the danger. Like a moth to a flame."

"You don't think I can change?"

"It's not a matter of change, Kell. You have an addiction. I've studied this. Thrill seeking is a heady narcotic."

He was quiet for a long stretch of time. "You know, a lot of education can be a dangerous thing, Jamie."

She quirked her mouth. "I know. It's made me boring, hasn't it?"

"No, just overly cautious. And I understand all your reasons. I do. But here's what I've been thinking. This is the last time I'm going to say this, so listen to me, okay?"

"I always do." Jamie waited for him to speak—and wondered how he did it. How did he sit there barefoot in the sand, with his pant legs rolled up and his knees bent, and still command the entire beach?

"Jamie, I have never walked away from you. And I am not going to now or in the future," he said, employing great deliberation with his words. "And you have never bored me. You've made me crazy, yes. Made me want to pull my hair out. You've excited me. Made me laugh. Made me cry. Made me want you. Made me want to wake up next to you every morning for the rest of my life. But you've never bored me. And you never will. I have changed in a lot of ways except one...in how much I love you. I don't know how to say it any plainer than that."

What an absolutely poignant and beautiful speech. Jamie sank to her knees in the sand. She held her arms out to Kell. "Hold me, please, Kell. Make love to me. Help me not to be so scared all the time."

In one easy and fluid motion, Kell sprang forward and tugged Jamie into his embrace. Together they fell back onto the sand, her on top of him, his arms around her. Her mouth found his and took it in a kiss of sheer need and desperation. When it ended, Jamie sat up, straddling his hips. Her hair was in her face, her palms were flat against Kell's chest. She gasped for air, finally getting her breath back. "I want to believe you, Kell. I do. I want to be able to say yes and to mean it. I want to know that this time, for all time, we can make it together."

Kell reached up and smoothed her hair back. He cupped her face in his strong, steady hands. "We can do this, Jamie. We can wake up tomorrow in Las Vegas."

"I want to believe that, Kell." It was the desire talking, the thick glaze of physical want, answering for her. She knew that…and didn't care, not at this moment. Jamie realized she was unbuttoning Kell's shirt while he was unbuttoning her blouse. Apparently, they were going to have sex right there, on the beach. Anyone could happen by. Surprising her was the realization that she didn't care. She was doing, not thinking. Because all she cared about was being with Kell in the most intimate sense of the word. And if what she was feeling was any indication, he really wanted her, too.

Kell helped her shrug out of her blouse. Under his deft and practiced touch, her bra soon followed. The night breeze caressed her bare breasts. Kell's warm hands quickly covered them and stroked their fullness. His thumbs flicked her swollen nipples. Delicious. Jamie arched her back, her face to the sky. Tiny sounds of pleasure escaped her. Kell's hands went to her waist as he bucked his hips against her soft and swollen mound.

He pulled her down to him. "You're wild, Jamie, absolutely wild. I've never seen you like this." His voice was deep, throaty...caressing. He smoothed his hands up her back and kneaded her skin, her shoulders.

Jamie captured his wide, firm lips in her kiss, daring his tongue to come out and spar with hers. He accepted her challenge, giving every bit as good as he got. She broke off their kiss, felt the heat rise between them, and lost to the moment, began pulling at his clothing as she slid down him. But when she sat up again on his thighs, a cry escaped him—not of pleasure, but of pain.

Jamie's cry followed his. "Your wound." She moved to get off him. "Ohmigod, Kell, I'm sorry."

He rose up a bit and clutched her by the arms. "Forget it. It's okay. It's just that the feeling is coming back. Never mind. Everything else is too good to worry about that."

Still, Jamie sat forward, trying to keep her weight off him. "Are you sure? I don't want to hurt you."

He lay back down on the sand and threw his arms out wide. His devilish chuckle met her words. "Oh, please...hurt me."

"Okay. But remember, you told me to," Jamie chirped...as she slid farther down Kell's body...until she could reach the zipper on his slacks. Underneath her hands he was as hard as granite. This night was magical for Jamie. And absolutely heady. Kellan was in her power every bit as much as she was in his. She had only to touch him and he was ready for her. She wanted to see just how ready.

Slowly, sensually, with one hand rubbing up and down his hard length, with her other hand she trailed his zipper down until his fly gaped open. "Hmm, what have we here," she teased as she freed his length from the restraint of his boxer shorts. "My, my...for me?"

Kell groaned and fisted his hands in the sand. Jamie chuckled...evilly. And took him in her mouth. She knew how to do this. Expertly. Kell had taught her. She'd never done this to another man. But she did it well. She was relentless...up, then down...fast, then slow...stroking, tasting, using her tongue to—

"Damn," Kell cried, jackknifing to a sitting position. "Come here."

Jamie did. And in an instant her wraparound skirt was in the sand, her panties beside it and she was positioning herself, with Kell's help, on top of him. "There," she moaned. "Right there."

Oh, the pulsing beat inside her body. It knew...it just knew. It sent its lubricating wetness to tell her she was ready. And she was. She was bursting with being ready. In the next instant she was sliding down on him. She'd meant to go torturously slow...but Kell would have none of that. Gripping her waist, with her hands flat against his chest, with her hair falling forward to shadow her face, Kell arched his hips and, in a flash of a moment, was deep inside her. She stilled, tensed, and cried out with the pleasure of it as he filled her. Kell's groan of joy matched hers. For eternal instants of time, neither one moved.

Then without a word or a sign, they were moving together. Jamie rode Kell as she would a horse...straddling him, matching his motions, feeling him all the way to her womb. Her muscles tensed around him, holding him inside her. Each stroke nearly sent her over the edge of sinful pleasure. She wanted it to last forever in the same moment that she wanted it to end gloriously. She didn't know what she wanted. She was beyond thought, beyond coherence. She rocked them toward a climactic release. Every nerve ending in her body seemed to find its way to the pleasuring center of her.

It was perfect.

Kell made a ragged sound at the back of his throat. He was very close. Jamie was, too. Wild abandon had overtaken excitement. Hard against him, she worked her pelvis in a deep back-and-forth movement. The pleasure was too intense. Jamie stilled, her breath was gone. "Now, Kell. Now."

"Anything you want, baby." Her desperate cry sent him into action. He gripped her waist and worked his powerful hips, pounding into her with all the strength and precision of a jackhammer, his tempo as unvarying as if he'd been a well-oiled machine.

The moment came. Jamie cried out her release—undulating wave after undulating wave of searing bliss. It drove Kell wild. He thrust almost brutally into her. Bearing down on him, she welcomed every inch of him...her mouth open, her head flung forward, her hair waving wildly. Her thighs tensed around his sides, she clung to him as if to a wildly bucking bronco.

In the next second...Kell met her in that place of abandonment of the senses and of rationality, and of perhaps even of a split second of unconsciousness where she couldn't even draw a breath. They hung there...on the ebbing tide of desire.

And then they collapsed. Under her cheek Kell's skin was hot and slick. His chest rapidly rose and fell with each breath. His heart beat in dull, thunderous claps under her ear. The crisp and curling hairs on his chest tickled her nose and lips. She didn't care. He held her tightly to him, a hand cupping her head, his other against the small of her back. Jamie had never felt more secure and protected—not to mention sated—in her life.

It was beautiful. Pure and perfect and whole. Surely no other couple in the history of love had ever achieved this perfect a union of body and soul.

"Jamie?" Kell's voice was warm in the night, her name a caress on his lips.

She smiled, loving how her name vibrated through his chest and against her ear. "Yes?"

"I want a whole lifetime of this with you. Babies. White picket fence. A big yard. Swings. Fighting about the kids and money. Suburbia. Long commutes. PTA. The hassle of bills. Hot nights. A life together. I want that."

That got her—for more than one reason. Tears pricked her eyes. Jamie sat up and looked down at Kell.

His gaze searched her face, and his expression sobered. "You're supposed to jump in and say you do too."

"I know," she murmured, not quite able to look him in the eye. "But I'm not sure I can give you that, Kell."

"Dammit. Here we go again."

# 11

AFTER THAT, Kell didn't say a word. He didn't move. He just lay under her and breathed...deeply and evenly.

Feeling as if she were shrinking inside, Jamie hated herself for her honesty. *Just marry the man, for heaven's sake, and worry about the rest of it later*, her feminine conscience railed at her. But she couldn't do that. Kell was too important to her to risk losing again. All she'd meant when she'd said she wasn't sure she could give him the life he wanted with her was that she felt he needed to be aware of the pitfalls of *her* life before deciding on a life together. *Well, gee, is that all? It's a wonder that any therapist ever gets married, Jamie Winslow, Ph.D.*

Kell moved to sit up and help Jamie off him. She retrieved her panties, shook the sand out of them, put them on, then arranged her clothes while he did the same. Then she sat next to him in the sand, suddenly feeling grittiness and the heavy humidity of the night wind.

Kell sat, looking out to sea. A muscle worked in his jaw. Jamie felt the chasm that had once again opened up between them. "The tide's coming in," he said absently. "I think we lost our shoes already."

"If not our minds and our modesty," Jamie added.

"Boy, our timing sucks, doesn't it?"

The anger in his voice shouldn't have surprised Jamie, but it did. With guilt pricking at her self-esteem, she picked at her skirt. "Yes. It always has."

Kell looked at her. "You have to give me something here, Jamie. Anything to give me a reason to keep trying with you. Because right now, I've got squat to sustain me. You keep telling me, in so many words, that love's not enough. All right, I believe you. Tell me why it isn't. Tell me what stands in its way."

"Our lives, Kell. The way we live them. Our differing expectations."

His chuckle was more of a grunt. "I was hoping you wouldn't have such a ready answer."

"It's the curse of my profession, all this analyzing."

"Analyze this—I love you, you love me, and everything else is details."

"That's exactly right. Long-term happiness for any couple lies in the details, Kell. Expectations, goals, like that. Differing ones can make or break even the best of relationships. That's what I'm trying to tell you."

"This sounds like marriage therapy before the marriage. But go ahead...give me some details for long-term happiness."

"All right. I'm going to get a lot of money for my book."

He shrugged. "So far *I'm* happy."

Despite herself, Jamie grinned. "I'm sure you are. But with that money comes tremendous responsibility. I have to travel and speak, be on TV and radio, be in the public eye, give interviews...things like that. They're in my contract."

"So? I wouldn't stop you. Hell, I'd be proud and would help in any way I could."

Jamie leaned over and kissed him. "You're sweet to say that. And I believe you. But there would be nothing for you to do but stand by. I mean, you can't help me write the book. And writing means a lot of time alone, too. Then I'd be off on those publicity tours. That means you could be pushed, emotionally and physically, to one side."

"Sounds like Melanie's life. She's left behind when Jeff is gone. She worries all the time, and there's not much he can do about it because he signed on for the danger in his life."

A frisson of excitement shot through Jamie. This was new. This was different—and good—on Kell's part. Finally he showed some understanding for things she'd been trying to tell him for years. "Go on," she said, hoping she didn't sound too much like a therapist.

"Well, I talked with Jeff the other night at the hospital about how they handle his absences and Melanie's fears."

"You did?" She was so proud of him.

"Yeah, I did." He grinned but sounded a bit defensive. "You're not the only one who thinks and worries, you know."

Jamie looked down at her hands. "I'm sorry, Kell. Is that how I come across?"

Kell wrapped an arm around her shoulders and lightly kissed her temple. "It's not your fault. I don't tell you what I'm thinking. And I'm sorry for that, Jamie. I'm beginning to see that my silent treatment gave you nowhere to go. And here I blew off your fear, thinking you wouldn't worry so much if I acted as if there was no reason for you to worry. Stupid, huh?''

"Not stupid. Just protective. It's kind of sweet in a way, I guess." Tears pricked Jamie's eyes. She wiped at them and sniffed. "That must have been some talk you had with Jeff."

Kell shrugged. "The talk was okay. But he made me think. He said there was nothing he could do about Melanie's fears except to tell her that we may go into dangerous hot spots, but it's our training and physical condition—the best in the world—that makes our missions successful and keeps us safe."

"But then there was this last mission when you both got hurt."

Guilt edged Kell's eyes. He exhaled sharply. "Yeah. Then there was this last mission." His jaw worked and he looked out toward the water. "It changed everything."

"I'm so sorry, Kell." Jamie grabbed a handful of sand and tossed it out in front of her. "Why does everything have to hit at once?"

Kell gave her his attention. "What's hit? What happened?"

"I heard from my agent today. She asked me how the writing is going. I had to tell her I hadn't even started. She was not amused and pretty much lectured me on self-discipline and told me I'd have to give up something for fame."

"Like what?"

"Well, she mentioned friends, family and society."

"Damn. That doesn't leave much."

Jamie met Kell's gaze. "That's what I said. And I just

don't want it to be us that I end up leaving behind. It's funny, you know. Now I'm in your position, in a sense, and I see how you feel. This is something I have to do, and all I can hope for is support and understanding. Yet, I really have no right to ask you to put yourself through it. Jeez, could it be harder?"

"I don't see how. But it sounds to me like I'm in the way, Jamie."

Jamie's heart hurt. She put a hand on his arm. A muscle flinched under her touch. "God, don't say that. I hate it."

"Me, too. But I think it's the truth."

Jamie gave in. "You're right. I can't say it isn't. I keep getting this picture of us as newlyweds trying to make a life together when one of us is always absent from the picture."

"Like movie stars."

"Exactly," Jamie grumbled. "And everyone knows *their* success rate with marriage."

"So what are you saying? We should wait until all the hype with your book settles down?"

"I'm not so sure it will settle down, or that I want it to. I mean, there would go my sales and my career. So, to make sure that doesn't happen, I'll be optioned to do another book after this one. Best-case scenario is...this is an ongoing thing, Kell."

"Ah, the life of a celebrity."

"Exactly. But this is what I want, Kell. Just like being a SEAL is what you want. I know you have a sense of duty. And I like that. In the same way, I'm very excited by all the possibilities open to me because I really think

I have something to say through my work. But right now, I'm more worried about you and me."

"So what do you want to do?" He was looking out to sea again.

Jamie drank in his profile...and the hard set of his jaw. She feared she was losing here. "I think we ought to think about what my career will mean for yours."

"Okay. Shoot."

"All right. For one thing, the publicity. You can't afford any, being a SEAL. So let's say this book goes as big as Highline Publishing thinks it will. There'll be some pretty heavy media interest about whoever I'm involved with."

He raised his eyebrows. "'Whoever?'"

"You know what I mean. Anyway, say that somehow we learn to handle the media. What worries me more is the amount of, well, let's call it *traveling* that you have to do."

He shrugged. "I have a desk job, remember? I'll be sitting right here." He poked a finger into the sand. The bitterness was there in his voice.

"Do you hear yourself? You won't sit at that desk for long, Kell, and we both know it. Say you're back out in the field in a year or two. I'm thinking...what if I'm home but you're gone? And then you're home and I'm gone? It's not like, with your military career, you could just pick up and follow me. I don't think you'd be happy for long doing that, even if you could...or would."

"Great. Dueling careers. Well, you've convinced me. Sorry I asked for forever." Resignation rang in his voice, but still, he reached over to stroke her back, his hand gently sliding up and down her spine.

Tender thrills of pleasure chased over Jamie's skin, making her words all that more heartfelt. "I hate this, Kell. All these years I've wanted you to settle down. And now, when you seem ready to do just that, I can't. My life is heating up and I'm the one getting ready to take all the chances. It's funny, isn't it?"

"Yeah. Hilarious."

Jamie brushed her hair back from her face and glanced over at Kell. His handsome profile was troubled. Fine lines creased his forehead. She tenderly stroked his clean-shaven cheek. "I do love you, Kell."

"I know," he said, not much above a whisper. "I guess this means we won't be waking up together in Las Vegas, right?"

"JAMIE, I swear I am about ready to get on a plane and fly to Tampa so I can pull all your hair out. God, you are so frustrating. I don't even know why Kell tries with you, little sister."

Jamie slumped onto her couch's cushions the next Monday morning as she listened to her sister's lecture...again. "I know. I just want everything to be perfect."

"Nothing is perfect, kiddo. Get over it. How old do you have to be before you realize that? I would have thought that this past weekend would have shown you that. I thought you learned something."

The events of the past forty-eight hours flitted through Jamie's consciousness. After leaving Kell, she and Donna had taken a trip they should have taken years ago. She swallowed. "I did. I learned to let go."

"Then act on that. Quit trying to think the future through, hon. Instead, grab an imperfect piece of it for yourself. Make the leap. Act. Don't think."

Kell's handsome face suddenly filled Jamie's mind. "That sounds like how Kell operates."

"Exactly. And the man gets things done, doesn't he? He has goals and he achieves them. Jamie, don't let this thing with Dad hold you back. It wasn't your fault he left. You have to know that. You may not have known it at thirteen, but you should now."

Jamie exhaled and shifted her position on the soft cushions under her. "I think I do, Donna."

"Good. Then quit making Kell pay for his part in that."

Jamie swallowed the lump on her throat. "Kell yelled that same thing at me several nights ago."

"Then listen to him. And to me." Donna's voice was pleading yet calm. Almost motherly. "Honey, I love you and I want to see you happy. And I know you love Kellan. So I'm just going to say this. Don't let that man slip through your fingers. Say yes to him."

Jamie couldn't say anything. She stared at the ceiling above her and watched it become a blur, thanks to her welling tears. A sniff escaped her.

"Look," Donna said, "I know you have to go to your therapy appointment, so I'll let you go. Just remember what I said, Jamie. You're going after your dreams in the other areas of your life, and I'm proud of you. That's good. But don't stop there. In this instance, lead with your heart. It's better than your mind. And everything else will follow. One action leads to another. Take that first step."

"So, YOU DIDN'T wake up in Las Vegas?" Dr. Hampton asked.

"Short answer...no. We'd probably still be there if we'd gone. That was just a couple of nights ago."

"I see. And how do you feel about not being there?"

"Like I broke a promise to a friend."

"I'm not sure I understand, Commander Chance."

Kell shrugged, downplaying his own comment. "It was nothing. I have a good friend who told me I should ask Jamie to marry me. I did. She wouldn't." He shrugged. "So I feel like I let him down."

"Him? Or yourself?"

Kell met the therapist's gaze. "Both, I guess." He sat upright, grimacing as he rubbed his leg.

"Does your thigh still hurt?"

"No."

"You were rubbing it as if it did."

"It's just sore. I got the stitches out a few days ago. The feeling's coming back to the nerves."

"That's a good sign. Then everything's healing as it should?"

"Yeah. It's fine."

"You mentioned your friend just a moment ago. Would that be Jeff, the one you said was in the hospital?"

"Yeah. Jeff's fine...well, better. He's still in the hospital, but at least up and around now."

"That's good news."

Kell grinned. "And his wife, Melanie, is expecting their first baby. They just found out."

"That's wonderful. You seem close to them."

"I am. I love Jeff like he's my brother. And Melanie…well, she's a sweetheart."

Dr. Hampton nodded and stared Kell's way…and waited. Kell had no idea what he was waiting for. But he had to call on his rigorous training to steel himself against the urge to squirm under this slight, bearded man's silent scrutiny. Finally, the silence got to Kell. "You okay, Doc?"

He nodded. "I am. I'm just wondering why you're here."

Kell made a broad gesture. "To talk, obviously."

"Of course. But it's my understanding from colleagues familiar with the Special Forces that you routinely undergo psychiatric evaluation out at the base."

"We do. It's as tough as the physical training. It's what keeps us safe. We don't go off half-cocked on a mission. It's all about being so damn good at what we do that we don't fail—" But he *had* failed. Kell lapsed into silence.

It wasn't lost on Dr. Hampton. "And yet sometimes thing go awry, don't they? Despite all the training and expertise."

"Yes. They do." Kell's words were terse, crisp—just the opposite of Dr. Hampton's quiet and soothing voice.

"And that's when you go in to talk to the psychiatrists at the base."

Suddenly this man was the enemy. "No. We have to

go in for debriefing after every mission, regardless of the outcome."

"I see. And you've been on many missions."

"Yes. What's your point?"

"My point, Commander Chance, is you should be used to answering questions about your feelings. And yet you're avoiding doing just that."

Kell shrugged. "I didn't think I was. But I don't talk to the military headshrinkers about things like this."

Dr. Hampton frowned. "So, what's the point?"

This was a subject he knew. Kell sat forward. "The point is to get cleared to go out on the next mission. You don't get cleared, you don't have a career."

"You feel passionately about this, don't you?"

"Hell, yes. Look, the service has spent millions of dollars on our training and equipment. We know that. And we have a mission. So we tell the shrinks we're fine. They tell our commanders we're fine. Everyone's happy, and we're back out in the field doing what it is we do best."

"I see. And what is that...what you do best?"

Kell sat back and quirked a corner of his mouth. "Well, I could tell you...but then I'd have to kill you."

Dr. Hampton's eyebrows shot up in alarm.

"Relax. It's just a joke. But seriously, most of my work is classified. I can't talk about it with you. See, I can talk about the missions with the military doctors, and how I feel about what I did and what happened. But not my personal feelings on other subjects. That's harder."

"Of course. Will you excuse me a moment? I need to write some of this down." Dr. Hampton spent the next few minutes making notes. Kell frowned and watched him—and fought the urge to lean forward to see what he was writing. Finally, the older man looked up at him. "Thank you. Now, let's talk about your personal feelings. How are you and Jamie doing now, today?"

Kell shrugged. "Fine."

Dr. Hampton eyed him. Then, with very precise movements, the psychiatrist put his notepad and pen on the low table next to him. He folded his hands in his lap and stared a hole through Kell. "That's the same evasive answer you just told me you give to the psychiatrists out at the base. You're wasting my time and your money, Commander."

Kell met the man's steady gaze...and saw a strength of will there that matched his own. He sighed and let loose his reticence. "All right. Point taken. Jamie and I aren't doing well at all. I don't think we're going to make it."

Kell watched Dr. Hampton assess him and then pick up his notepad and pen. Surprising to Kell was how relieved he was that the man had. "So," the doctor said. "Tell me why you think that you won't make it."

"Because she won't marry me. That would be closure, wouldn't it, if we got married?"

"Well, certainly. But only if it was for the right reason."

"Which would be for love, right?"

"Yes, I suppose. But a lot of times, two people—"

"Look, I don't want to hear any buts. I love her and she loves me. Yet she won't marry me. I even proposed to her on a moonlit beach and we made love and she still said no. What's wrong with two people, Doc, who make love and then fight right after?"

"Nothing. It's entirely normal. It's a way of reestablishing boundaries following such intense intimacy."

Kell nodded. "I see. Like personal space."

"Exactly."

"Well, she's getting plenty now. Stupidly I told her last Friday that if she didn't give me a yes then, I was rescinding my proposal."

"I see. And did you?"

Kell shrugged. "Not really. But now she's turned it around on me. I haven't heard a word from her since Friday. She won't take my calls or answer her buzzer to let me in when I go over to her place. I've called her friends. They tell me they haven't heard from her. It may be true, but the bottom line remains I'm shut off. What the hell am I supposed to think, Doc? What should I do?"

"Are you asking me?"

"Hell yes, I am. Right now you're my only link to her. You're the only one who can tell me what she's thinking."

A look of censure came over the older man's face. "Oh, I'm afraid you're misinformed, Commander Chance. I can't tell you anything about Jamie's state of mind. That's privileged information. All we—you and I—can and will talk about is *your* state of mind."

"Well, my state of mind is tied up in hers. And she won't see me or talk to me. So that leaves me where?"

"I don't know. I can't say."

"That's two different conclusions, Dr. Hampton."

"You're right. Allow me to rephrase it. I can't say because I don't know what her state of mind is right now."

Kell nodded and eyed the man as he mulled that over. "Then she hasn't been in and you haven't talked to her since last week, right?"

"I can't tell you that, either. I'm sorry."

Frustration ate at Kell. About ready to give up, he sat forward and ran a hand through his hair. "I'm not trying to put you on the spot, Dr. Hampton. It's just that I feel so helpless. I love her. She loves me. When we're together it's magic. We have fun. We laugh. I've even begun to let her in, to see how I think. She says she loves that, that it's progress. Then she says no and locks me out. What the hell is going on? What does that indicate to you?"

"A lot of things, actually. But answer this for me. Did you and Jamie try what I suggested?"

Kell chuckled. "Yes, we tried. For about ten minutes. But the chemistry got in the way...more than once."

Dr. Hampton cleared his throat. "I see. Well, then what happens...once the chemistry is sated?"

"We talk a bit. Establish some common ground. Then we leave it at that. And one of us walks out. Usually her."

Dr. Hampton nodded and stroked his beard...and appeared to be doing a lot of thinking.

"Tell me something, Doctor." Dr. Hampton met Kell's gaze. "Is this normal? I mean for a person with a Ph.D. in psychology. Shouldn't she be, uh, better at relationships?"

"Well, it's not at all unusual in the field, if that's what you're asking. As counselors—and Jamie is a superb one, from what I've observed—we tend not to apply our expertise to our own relationships, I'm afraid. As if we don't want to take the job home. There's nothing worse for a couple than for one to constantly be evaluating the other one. It causes the other person to feel manipulated. So, when it comes to our own personal relationships, we tend to be as, well, clueless as the untrained person is."

"I see your point. It's hard to be objective when you're in the middle of something that's tied up in your emotions."

"Very well said."

"Thanks. But I didn't mean to imply that I think Jamie wouldn't be good at her profession. She's the smartest person I know. And she cares a lot about everything."

"That's been my experience with her, too. She's very passionate about life and how it should be lived." Dr. Hampton then surprised Kell by looking at him in a thoughtfully assessing manner. "She's also very passionate about you."

Kell felt as if his heart was on his sleeve. "She is? Then you think there's a chance she'll come around and make a commitment to me?"

"Why is that so important to you? I mean right now, today."

Kell gestured his frustration. "Because I love her. I always have, no matter what, no matter how many times she's walked away. I've always believed that if you loved someone, you should marry them and have a life together. Isn't that the way it's supposed to be?"

"Certainly."

Kell wanted to jump up and scream. "Then, dammit, tell me what's wrong here. I've been talking to her, letting her inside my head—and that is not an easy thing for me to do. I just want all of her, Doc, and I'm willing to put myself on the line for that. Why is that so awful?"

"I don't think it's awful at all. I think it's wonderful. But I also think that the problem may not be with you."

"Which means it's with Jamie?"

Dr. Hampton's smile was sympathetic. "I think so. But I've already said more than I should."

"No, you haven't said near enough." Kell wanted to give up. "She won't see me or talk to me. Do you see my problem? Where do I go from here?"

Dr. Hampton studied Kell a moment and then looked at his watch. "You have about five minutes left in your hour, Commander."

Hope fled. Kell started to get up. "Keep them for yourself, Doc. Have a cup of coffee on me. I'm through here."

"Sit down, Commander Chance." When Kell did, he said, "Thank you. I've been listening to you and watching you. I've watched you with Jamie, too. I believe you when you say that you love her. And I know she loves you. And even though I'm not supposed to, well, say or do anything—and I'm not going to—I do also have a special interest in Jamie. She's a wonderful young woman, and I would love to see her happy."

"Me, too." Excited anticipation, of the same sort that gripped Kell before a deployment, now tightened his stomach. Finally, something he understood. A mission...and Jamie was the target. A moving target. "So what are you saying?"

"I'm saying that by chance, pure and simple, my next client...were you to talk longer than you should and go over your hour...would be someone you'd run into anyway as you were leaving my office. And it could turn out that you know her, too."

Kell grinned. "Dr. Hampton, you're a stand-up guy."

The older man smiled. "Thank you. And now I'm going to ask you to be one, too, not that you haven't been. But what I want you to do—providing Jamie consents to speak with you—is to promise to use the time productively. Talk. No raised voices. No accusations. A lot of listening. And no touching. Can you do that? I want you to think about it before you answer because this will be a lot of work."

Kell thought he already knew his answer. So it surprised him to realize that he did have some questions, some doubts. Did he want to continue to knock his head against the brick wall that was Jamie's resistance? Was it hopeless? He had to ask himself what he was getting out of all this. Was he happy? Was she? Would she give him a sign that she wanted it to work out this time?

Suddenly, it occurred to him that she must want it to, or she wouldn't keep coming back to him. She wouldn't be so upset that they couldn't work it out. So the truth was...she couldn't walk away from him any more than he could walk away from her. Moths to a flame, she'd said. Well, maybe they could learn to control that fire and use it to their advantage.

Kell nodded. "Okay. I've thought about it. And I want to do this."

Dr. Hampton grinned broadly. "Excellent, Commander." He put down his notepad and pen. "Now then, what do you want to talk about for the next few minutes?"

With excitement and hope coursing through him, Kell crossed his arms over his chest and looked around the diploma-laden office walls. Nothing to talk about there—nothing that he'd understand. He checked the clock hanging on the wall. Five minutes. "So, how about those Buccaneers, huh? Think they've got a shot at the Super Bowl this year, Doc?"

# 12

THOUGH TIRED and burned-out emotionally, Jamie sat idly thumbing through a dog-eared magazine while she chatted with Roberta, Dr. Hampton's grandmotherly secretary. The door to the inner office opened and Dr. Hampton appeared. He smiled at her and raised a hand in silent greeting. Jamie smiled back and opened her mouth to speak...then stopped. Because standing beside Dr. Hampton was the *last* person she needed to see right now. Kellan Chance.

The two men, Dr. Hampton and Kell, stood there looking guilty—in Jamie's estimation—as they glanced around the room. She couldn't believe this! This was *her* haven, not his. This felt like a betrayal on both their parts.

Roberta broke the silence. "Your next appointment is here, Dr. Hampton."

Suddenly Jamie realized she was standing. At some point, she'd dropped the magazine, which lay now at her feet. Almost involuntarily, Jamie's hands fisted at her sides. She stared at the two men. "How did this happen?"

"He made an appointment," Roberta supplied helpfully. "We had a cancellation."

Everybody stared at the gray-haired secretary.

Dr. Hampton gestured to Jamie and then Kell. "Why

don't the both of you come into my office? We can talk in there."

Jamie glared at him. "You bet we can." Jamie stormed toward the two men at full steam. Wordlessly, they parted for her and allowed her to precede them into the low-lit and soothing atmosphere of Dr. Hampton's treatment room. He closed the door behind them.

Jamie whipped around. "I'm not sitting on that couch with *him*." Her pointing finger stabbed the air in Kell's direction. Kell pulled back, looking offended.

Dr. Hampton held up a hand. "No one is asking you to do that, Jamie. Sit where you please. And I must say that your anger seems a bit out of proportion here, more so than the situation warrants."

Stung, Jamie's posture stiffened. "Maybe my anger level does seem inappropriate to you, Dr. Hampton. And you could be right. But it is an honest emotion. And the truth is, I am angry. Very angry."

"I see." Dr. Hampton waved her to the plushly upholstered chair behind her and Kell to the couch. When they were all seated, Dr. Hampton leaned toward Jamie. "Do you want to tell me why you're angry?"

Jamie's gaze betrayed her by going to Kell. Dr. Hampton obviously noticed. "Do you wish for Commander Chance to leave?"

Suddenly realizing how obnoxious she was acting, Jamie shook her head. "No. He can stay."

Kell settled back on the couch. Both men focused on her, waiting for her to explain. Jamie found she couldn't. She didn't know where to start. How to start. She feared that tears would soon well in her eyes.

"Jamie?" Dr. Hampton prompted.

"I'm sorry," she said. "I was...gathering my thoughts." It wasn't true, but she didn't feel she was ready to talk about her weekend yet. Or her phone conversation today with Donna. So she went with the situation before her. "It just surprised me to see Kell here and to know that he was talking to you." Jamie crossed her legs. "I reacted badly, I know. But I couldn't help feeling the same way I did as a little girl, when someone had snitched on me to my mother."

"That's not the case here, Jamie."

"Maybe not," she said, including them both. "But that's how it felt. As if I'd walked into a setup."

"Well, it's not," Kell answered, his expression earnest. "Roberta had a cancellation and put me in that time slot. You heard her. It was pure chance that it would be the hour before your appointment. And Dr. Hampton didn't know I was on his schedule until he saw me."

Her gaze locked with Kell's. "I understand all that. But did you know I was coming in today?"

"Now, how would I know?" was Kell's first response. But then his glance slid from her to Dr. Hampton. Jamie followed his direction and saw Dr. Hampton nod. She narrowed her eyes. Something was definitely up. Kell caught her gaze. "All right, I did know—but not until the very end of my session. I ran over my hour, and there you were. Hell, I didn't even know I was coming in today until I decided this morning to call."

"Why did you call?"

Kell ran a hand through his hair and exhaled. "I admit I wanted Dr. Hampton to talk to me about what you're feeling, but he wouldn't. He told me plainly enough that he and I could only talk about me...and how I feel about you."

"Really?" Well, that took the wind out of her sails. Suddenly it was hard to hold on to her anger, no matter its cause. Kell was so darned vulnerable looking right now, so wounded. Like her. Jamie lowered her gaze to her upholstered chair's arm and, with a finger, traced the floral pattern she found there. "And what did you tell him...about how you feel about me?"

"I told him the truth." Kell's voice rang with the conviction of his words. Jamie looked up at him. His black eyes were compelling. "That I love you and I can't get through to you. That no matter what I do, it's wrong. That I don't know how to make you happy...and that maybe I should just stop trying."

Jamie's heart lurched. "Oh, please don't stop trying, Kell. I don't want you to do that."

Kell leaned forward, his forearms resting on his thighs. "Then what *do* you want, Jamie? Tell me what to do. I feel like I'm the only one trying here. Like I'm jumping through flaming hoops and you keep adding more with a bigger fire."

Dr. Hampton chose to break in. "Jamie, Kell, if you'll excuse me..." He stood up. "I just remembered something I have to do that might take a while. I know this is highly irregular, but do you two think you can talk alone for a bit?"

Though a little startled, Jamie's answer was automatic. "Sure."

"Good." He turned to Kell. "Commander? Are you comfortable with that?"

"I am." Kell never looked away from Jamie as he answered.

She couldn't take her eyes off him, either. Every line in Kell's body radiated a passionate intensity that made her breath catch. Suddenly she wanted Dr. Hampton gone so she could hear what Kell had to say. Whatever it was, it promised to be exciting. She thought again of Donna's advice. *Quit thinking and act. Listen to you heart and not your head.* A sudden giddiness raced through Jamie. She licked her lips.

"Excellent," Dr. Hampton said. "I wouldn't normally do this, of course. But I feel that with Jamie's credentials, she will take the appropriate steps to see that things don't get out of hand. However, should things get uncomfortable for either one of you—"

"We got it, Doc." Kell's voice was sharp. "We'll be fine. You can go now."

Jamie understood the urgency that lay behind Kell's words. She looked at her therapist. "We'll be okay, Dr. Hampton. Take your time."

He smiled and nodded, then turned around and left the room. They were alone now. Jamie crossed her arms and stared hard at the handsome man she loved so very much. "He was just giving us a chance to talk, I guess. After all, I was his next appointment."

"So it would seem." Kell stared at her, his black eyes glittering.

Jamie couldn't deny that her heart was thumping erratically. Nor could she deny that all she wanted to do was fling herself into Kell's arms and tell him what had happened over the weekend. She wanted to tell him how much she loved him and how much she needed him to hold her right now.

"Truce?" Kell said suddenly.

"Truce," she agreed. *Go for your dream, Jamie. Make that man yours.*

Kell leaned forward on the couch, running a hand through his hair, and said nothing. As always, he was fascinating for Jamie to watch. She tried to be detached but failed, consoling herself with the realization that Kell's presence in any room commanded attention. Still, she waited for him to speak. "You look tired. You okay?"

Was she okay? She didn't know. But then she thought about it. "Yeah. I'm okay. I really am—maybe for the first time in a long time. How about you?"

"I'm good. You sure you're all right? You're giving off some weird vibes, Jamie."

Jamie quirked her mouth. "I said I was fine, and I am." If he kept this up, she'd be crying. And she really didn't want to do that. She felt she'd done enough crying over the weekend to last her a lifetime.

Kell looked around the room awkwardly. "This isn't going the way I had hoped."

"Things in life rarely do. For anyone."

He exhaled, then looked back at her. "That's true. We always manage to screw up even the best of things, don't we? All I know is I don't want to walk out of this room until we have that damn closure thing, one way or the other."

Jamie swallowed, felt the betraying prick of tears in her eyes. She wasn't sure she could do this today. She wasn't sure she could face another loss. But it looked as if Kell wasn't giving her much choice. "Go on."

"All right." He sat forward, his expression intense. "We've been trying for two weeks now to see if this thing between us is going to work. And all we've managed to accomplish is great sex—which I'm totally on board with. But still, everything else is killing me. It's like I can have you physically, but not emotionally."

Jamie frowned. "That's what I say about you."

Kell sat back, crossing his legs and with his arms spread across the sofa's spine. "I know. So when did we both get to be such tight-asses?"

Jamie blinked. "I hadn't thought of myself that way. Donna thinks I need to get over it and do something. Chase my dreams and get them."

"Good advice. I've always liked Donna."

Jamie smiled. "Me, too."

"I like you, too, Jamie. I think you should know that."

That got to her. "I like you, too, Kell. This sounds like a junior-high conversation. You know, like passing notes that said 'check here if you like me.'"

A corner of Kell's mouth quirked up in amusement. "We actually did that in junior high, remember?" His dark eyes glittered. "I checked that I like you. Nothing's changed. I liked you long before I loved you, Jamie. I think that's important for us to remember."

"I do, too, Kell. We were friends first and cared about each other with a different sort of passion. I loved that feeling, didn't you? I could always count on you for anything. You were always there."

"I still am, Jamie. Just as you are for me. You were a

little girl with pigtails who trailed after me and annoyed the hell out of me. And I couldn't have loved you more. I have always needed you, even when I couldn't say it to you or even admit it to myself."

Jamie's defenses melted. She felt warm all over, liquid, vulnerable. "Oh, Kell." She raked her hands through her hair. "I just want everything else, all the stupid thinking and doubting and worrying I do to just go away. God, I just want to be happy."

Kell hadn't moved, but he seemed closer to her. "I want that, too, Jamie. I just don't know how to get us there. Do you?"

Jamie stared into his eyes, then found herself noting the little things...like how his watch fit his wrist, how manicured his nails were, how he sat. She looked again into those black eyes of his. "I don't know anything anymore, Kell. I'm just damn tired of myself and my own thoughts."

"Well, lucky for you, I never am."

"I don't know why you're not. I give you nothing."

"You give me everything." Kell pointedly looked around the room they were in and indicated it with a sweep of his hand. "We're in a psychiatrist's office. And you're a psychologist." His grin was warm and infectious. "Let's just talk, see where we go, where we end up. What do you say?"

Jamie answered his smile with one of her own. "I say yes."

Yes. It was a first for her. A hopeful first. Suddenly, she began to feel as if she meant it, too.

KELL WATCHED JAMIE...that sweet face he saw every night in his dreams and wanted to see every morning when he woke up. That was his goal, his targeted end. How to start? "So, Jamie, you made quite the impression on Jeff and Melanie."

Her eyes rounded. "I did? Good or bad."

"Good. Come on, you know you never make a bad impression on people."

"No, I don't know that. But I'm glad to hear it." Her expression changed, became curious. "So...what'd they say?"

Kell chuckled. This was the Jamie he loved. And, God, how he loved her. "Well, Jeff wouldn't let me leave his hospital room until I promised to ask you to marry me."

Jamie's face colored. "Why in the world did he do that?"

She put a hand to her chest. Kell noticed how her pink blouse snugly fit her full breasts. He was sure he could smell the warm, sweet scent of chemistry between her perfume and the skin in the intimate space of her cleavage. He forced himself to meet her waiting gaze. "Right now he thinks the whole world should take the day off, find itself a nice woman and settle down."

"Well, that's a good philosophy."

"He thinks so. Probably because he's happily married and about to be a father."

Jamie smiled brightly. "Yes, Melanie told me. How exciting! She said they'd been trying for five years."

"Yeah. So, what else did Melanie tell you the other day at the hospital?"

"She told me...about you."

Not sure how he felt about that, Kell sat back on the couch "I see. That had to be fun."

"Fun, no. Informative, yes."

"Great. I feel like I'm about to be skewered on a barbecue spit."

"It's not as bad as all that."

"Make me believe you." He patted the seat cushion next to him. "Care to join me?"

She looked from his face, to the cushion, and back to him.

"I promise to behave," he assured her, again noting, and wondering about, the tired lines that bracketed her mouth. Something was very wrong with her. Silently, he watched her get up and cross the space between them. She sat down...not too close, not too far away. He studied her up close. She looked pale, sad...like she'd gotten bad news. He opened his mouth to question her again, but she spoke first.

"Okay, about my talk with Melanie," she said. Despite his worry about her, Kell's gaze seemed to stray to her legs...long, tan, muscled from her jogging. "Kell?"

He jerked his gaze up to her face. "I'm listening."

"Sure you are. But, anyway, Melanie..." Jamie got a faraway look on her face as if she was ordering her thoughts. Then she focused on him again. "Okay. I suppose she talked more about the mission than anything. Don't be mad at her. Her husband was there, too."

Kell's jaw tensed. "I'm painfully aware that Jeff was there. Go on."

"Well, she told me about things you really could

have told me, Kell. And I wish you had. I wish you felt as if you could trust me with things the way you trust her."

Duly chastised, Kell reached over and took Jamie's hand in his. Her heart was in her big blue eyes. "All right." He rested his head against the couch's spine and closed his eyes. After a few moments of difficult silence, he began talking. "There were five of us. We'd been there three days. We'd parachuted in, then lived off the land, making our way to our target at night, skulking through the woods, sleeping in shifts during the day. The usual stuff. That third night there, we approached our objective and set the explosives. Then all hell broke loose. They were on to us, about twenty of them, armed to the teeth. We had to fight our way out, radio the helicopter that we were under fire—and still blow up the munitions plant."

He opened his eyes and rolled his head until he was looking at her. Her face was a bit paler now. "You didn't hear that." She shook her head. He then assumed his former position...head back, eyes closed. "Anyway, we blew up the target and I got hit with flying debris—"

"The cut on your thigh?"

His answer was a nod. "I went down. Jeff grabbed me up and was helping me limp away while the other guys were covering us. We went around a corner—right into a nest of bad guys. Long story short, Jeff shielded me and took a couple of bullets meant for me. It damn near killed him."

"And you."

There was a catch in her voice. Kell opened his eyes

and looked over at her. Tears were rolling down her cheeks. He reached up to wipe them away. "Hey, it's okay," he told her. "I'm all right, and I'm right here."

She smacked at his chest. "Dammit, Kell, you could have been killed." Her voice, though muffled a bit by his shirt, was ragged. "You have to stop doing that. You just have to."

Feeling more content and calm than he had in weeks—Jamie was here, that was all he needed—Kell rubbed her back. "I keep telling you that I have, Jamie." He pulled her up so he could see her face. Her troubled expression had Kell's heart turning over with poignant tenderness. "Honey, remember that desk job I told you about? It's the truth. There's no more going back into the field for me. Or Jeff, if I get my way."

"What do you mean?"

"Jeff wants to come in out of the field. I'm looking into making him my second-in-command."

"Oh, Kell, that is wonderful. Melanie will be so glad."

"Yeah, Jeff, too. He's tired of the grind of being a field operative. Who could blame him? He almost had his butt shot off. Right now that's in his favor. He's not in peak physical condition and may never be again after this last complication—"

Jamie had grabbed his arm. "Oh God, don't tell me—did something else happen?"

"No. I'm talking about his last setback. Anyway, he's going to take a while to heal. So the best use of his training and skills would be in my office. We'll be hell on wheels with all the bureaucracy—the paper pushing and budgets and strategy meetings. Picture that—

middle management in the military world. Actually, I'm beginning to think it will be pretty exciting to be in a position to have the big picture finally, instead of being stuck in a muddy ditch somewhere halfway around the world and wondering why I'm there."

Jamie nodded. "I hope it works out for Jeff and Melanie. And for your sake."

Her voice was flat. Kell was getting more and more worried. "My sake? Why mine?"

"Because Jeff means a lot to you. Kind of like your brothers."

Kell nodded. "Yeah, he does." Then he rubbed at his injured thigh and chuckled. "Hell, Brandon and T.J. would take one look at this scratch on my thigh and laugh, wouldn't they?"

Jamie shook her head. "No, they wouldn't. Mom told me that she talked to your mom. She said your mother told her that they were both pretty upset about it."

Kell sank back on the cushions. "Yeah, I know. They called me, too."

"You don't sound like that went so well."

Kell turned to look up at her. "Actually, it did. Both calls. I expected them to be, I don't know, disappointed in me somehow."

Jamie shoved at his shoulder. "Kell, for God's sake, they're your brothers. You don't have to blow yourself up to make them care about you."

He grunted. "That's pretty much what they said. It was dumb of me to worry about what they'd think. I was getting the chip on my shoulder about it, though."

"And now?"

Kell grinned up at her. "Well, Ms. Counselor, I think I'm okay with them. And with me. How about you? Are you okay with me?"

Jamie looked down at her lap. "I am." Then she took a deep breath, as if she was trying to find the courage to say something to him.

"Jamie?" Kell prompted. "What is it?"

She looked over at him. "My mother says hello. I talked to her last night. About a lot of things." Jamie's gaze shifted away from him. "She...asked me if I was going to be alone. And I told her no, that I'd call you."

Kell sat up straighter on the couch. Alarm bells were going off inside him. "But you didn't call me. And why would your mother suddenly be worried about you being alone? What's going on, Jamie?"

She stared at him...hollow-eyed. "I meant to call you. I did. I just...fell asleep after I talked to her. It was late."

Kell raked a hand through his hair. "I don't get any of this, Jamie."

"I know."

"Then tell me. Look, when I took you home Friday night from the beach, we kissed and said we'd talk the next day. So I didn't think anything was wrong. Then I spent all weekend trying to reach you. But you wouldn't take my calls."

A stricken look came over her face. "It wasn't that I wouldn't take them, Kell. I wasn't there to take them."

"Well, where were you?"

She took a deep breath. "I left early Saturday morning and was gone all weekend. I just got back last night."

Kell looked at her as if he'd never seen her before. "You just—? Where'd you go? You never said anything on Friday about having to go somewhere."

"I know." She looked down at her lap silently. Unheeded seconds ticked by. Jamie's face grew pale. Finally, she raised her head. "I didn't say anything because I didn't know, myself, until it happened. And then when it did, I couldn't talk to you. I just couldn't. Not until it was over."

Kell's heart pounded against his ribs. "Hell, Jamie. What is it?" Her blue eyes were swimming with tears. Kell took her hands in his. "You're scaring me. What's wrong? Just tell me."

"It's my father."

# 13

KELL WENT cold inside. "Your father? What about
him?"

Jamie breathed in and out deeply several times as if
she was having trouble catching her breath. Kell was
dying inside but all he could do was wait for her.
"He's...gone," Jamie finally said raggedly. "Dead.
About five years ago. A car wreck."

"Jesus." Kell felt as if his blood had drained out of
him. "Jamie, do you want me to get Dr. Hampton back
in here? Oh hell—that's why you came in today, isn't
it? And then I—" With the heel of his hand, he
smacked himself in the forehead. "What a self-serving
jerk I am."

She recaptured his hand in hers. "Don't say that.
You didn't know. And, yes, I came in today to talk with
Dr. Hampton about this—and you. But right now, I
think I'd rather just talk to you."

Warmed by her admission that she needed him, Kell
rubbed her arm. "All right. You poor kid. How'd you
find out...about your father?"

"Mom told me. When I got home last Friday after
our date, she'd left me a message to call her, no matter
how late. I did...and she told me." Jamie took another
deep breath, as if for courage. "You'll love this. He'd
remarried. His widow just found some old box of stuff

he'd evidently kept hidden away. She was cleaning out her house, getting ready to move, and found it. He had pictures of Donna and me, and other silly things he'd kept. But Mother's address was on one of Donna's report cards, I believe. So she looked Mother up and called her."

"Yikes. How'd that go over?"

"Apparently better than I would have ever guessed. Mom sounded pretty okay with everything, believe it or not. That surprised me."

Kell nodded. "Maybe she was more over it—him— than she'd realized."

"I think you're right. As awful as it must have been for her to hear from this woman, I think it showed her just how far she'd come. So, I'm glad for that."

"Well, that's good then. What happened next?"

Jamie met and held his gaze. "I went to get the box."

"What?" Adrenaline shot through Kell. "You went to get the box? Where? Were you alone? I would have gone with you if you'd asked me, Jamie. I—"

"No." She'd put her fingers over his mouth to quiet him. "I wanted more than anything for you to be with me, but I had to do this alone." She lowered her hand, again holding his. "I couldn't make myself call you, Kell. If I'd heard your voice, I would have shattered. It seemed important right then that I stay numb in order to get through everything. Can you understand that?"

Kell ached inside for her. "God, Jamie. Of course I understand."

Relief flooded her expression. "Thank God. But I didn't go alone. Donna met me there. She left Wayne and the kids at home and flew to South Dakota. That's where my father had been living. Well, anyway, when we got there, we visited his..." She took a deep breath. "His grave. And took some flowers."

Jamie stopped talking and just sat there.

Kell watched her a moment and then thought it best that he pull her out of whatever it was she was seeing inside her head. "Man, what you've been through, Jamie."

Jamie nodded, seemed to be more herself. "Actually, it wasn't awful. The lady was really nice. Apologetic. Her name is Helen. Red hair. Sweet. No kids. She said she would have let us know sooner...but my father never talked about us. So she had no idea we existed." Jamie drew in another deep breath before continuing. Kell's heart ached for her. She was going through mental hell and there wasn't a thing he could do to take it away from her. "Anyway, Helen gave us her new address. She's moving—you'll love the irony of this—to Las Vegas to live with her sister."

Kell dared to chuckle. "No way. You're making that up."

Jamie finally smiled. "I'm not. Everybody ends up in Las Vegas but us. Go figure."

"So you think you'll keep in touch with her?"

Jamie shrugged. "I didn't at first. But you know, Kell, I think I just might. I thought all the way up there that I didn't want to know anything about him since he obviously didn't care about us. But I think he did in his own way, whatever it was. I mean, I saw all the things he'd kept. There was even a picture of him and Mom together."

"Where's all that stuff now?"

"I have some of it. Donna kept some and took a few things for Mom to keep."

"That was nice." Kell felt compelled to speak his mind. "I can't pretend to understand your father, Jamie. Normal people don't do what he did. You think he had some kind of mental breakdown back then that preceded his just up and leaving his family like he did?"

Jamie shook her head. "No. Mom says they were never right together. She was pregnant with Donna when they married. Mom thinks Dad never loved her but that he tried to do the right thing. Then, after a while, he just couldn't keep pretending. It's all so sad. You know, sometimes I think I accepted this offer here in Tampa because the only time the family seemed happy was when my father was stationed at MacDill. Maybe I was trying, without realizing it, to recapture that time."

"Makes sense."

Jamie frowned. "Kell, do you think I'd be awful if I wanted to know more about my father? I mean like talking to Helen later on."

Kell rubbed her hands with his thumbs. "No, I don't think you'd be awful. But do you think your mother would be okay with that?"

"I'd ask her first, of course. But I don't think it would be a problem. In fact, she's the one who encouraged us to go up there and talk to Dad's...wife." Jamie's smile was wounded. "I can't call her my stepmother. I just can't."

"No one says you have to. But your mom has a great attitude about this. She gets my respect."

"Mine, too. Especially since my father never paid her a penny in child support." Jamie suddenly became animated. Her color returned. Her eyes looked brighter. "Kell, that's why this book deal is so important to me. It's about the money. I want to give my mother everything she never had. I want somehow to pay her back for all the sacrifices she made for me and Donna. I want her to really live it up. Quit her job if she wants. Pay off the house. Go anywhere she pleases. That's very important to me. She's always been there, no matter what. Never complaining. If I could only, one day, be half the woman she is, Kell, I'd be happy."

Kell stroked Jamie's cheek. "I don't think I've ever loved you more than I do at this moment, Jamie. And I think your mother would agree with me when I say that you're already one hell of a woman. And her equal in every way."

Suddenly shy, Jamie lowered her gaze. "You're just being sweet, Kell."

"Hardly." Sitting there, looking at her, with her close enough that he could feel the heat from her body, Kell thought about it—and knew what he had to say. "Jamie, since I had all that time over the weekend to myself, I did some thinking about us. And I came to realize that I've been unfairly pushing you to get you to commit. Well, no more. Things happen in their own time...or they don't. If it happens for us, then it happens. And if it doesn't...I'll just go off somewhere and die." He grinned to show her he was kidding. But he knew the truth—he would die if she pushed him away.

Jamie's eyes filled with tears. "Don't ever say that again. I need you alive."

With those words, Jamie flung herself into his arms, and nuzzled her face against his throat. "I love you so much, Kell," she murmured. "Hold me. I've wanted all weekend for you to hold me."

And Kell held her—tight. This was the most perfect moment of his life, he told himself. Jamie was here and in his arms. He'd opened up to her. She'd opened up to him. They could do this. He began to believe.

Jamie stayed so still and silent in his arms that Kell began to wonder if she'd gone to sleep. If she had, it wouldn't be any wonder. She'd had the weekend from hell. Kell shifted her in his arms, settling her more across his lap, holding her as he would a child. With her head resting against his shoulder, he rubbed her leg and back in a comforting way. "I love you, baby."

Jamie pulled back. "You're all I've ever wanted, Kell. I love you, too. And I have something else to tell you. I talked to my agent this morning. I asked Liz about the amount of publicity and travel I'd have to do. And guess what? It's not all the time. It's pretty much just when the book hits the stands. She assures me I'll have lots of downtime for writing and not everything Highline Publishing is planning will require my actual presence. And things like radio interviews I can do from home. So it's not as bad as I feared. Which makes me feel better."

"Me, too. With my new job, I'll be pretty settled. And the more I think about it, I think it's just what I need." Kell was very aware that they were saying a lot—and pretty much talking around a subject they hadn't named. He grinned at Jamie. "Are we dangerously close to a closure here, or is it just me?"

Jamie's expression cleared. Humor sparked in her blue eyes. "It's not just you. I feel it, too." She grinned in such a way that left Kell no doubts about what her next words would be. "Make love to me."

Such a startling change in her. Gone was the needy girl. Here was the seductive woman. A sharp thrill of desire jetted through Kell—in the same instant that reality set in. "What? Here?"

"Yes." She nibbled kisses up the column of his neck. "Right here." Then, she rubbed her hand over his chest, kneading his muscles. Taking his hand, she smoothed it up under her skirt. "I've wanted you— needed you—all weekend. Love me, Kell. Don't make me beg."

To his own startlement, Kell realized he was appalled. "I don't want you to beg. And, Jamie, honey, nothing would make me happier than to— Stop that." She'd arched her back, pushing her breasts up against him. Kell's breathing quickened. He had only a few moments left in which to restore sanity before she drove him over the edge she—and he—so obviously wanted. He grabbed her hands. "Do you remember where we are? Dr. Hampton could open that door and come in at any moment. That could be disastrous."

Jamie sobered. "You're right."

Finally. That had been close. Kell exhaled and released her hands.

Her expression giving nothing away, Jamie looked into his eyes. "Will you excuse me a minute?"

He wasn't sure he trusted her, but he shrugged. "Sure."

"Thank you." She slid off his lap and, while unbuttoning her blouse and slipping out of her shoes, crossed the room.

*I'm a dead man,* Kell thought as he watched her.

Now at the door, Jamie pushed in the lock button on the doorknob. Kell's eyes widened. Jamie whipped around to face him and leaned her back against the door. Her expression was absolutely devilish. "Problem solved."

"No, the problem is just now beginning, Jamie." He tried to sound upset...still he was so damn turned on at the prospect of this bit of risky business.... "What the hell do you think you're doing?"

She planted her hands at her waist—which caused her unbuttoned blouse to gape open—and gave him a breathtaking view of her full breasts straining against her lacy bra. "Taking chances. Letting go. Trying not to be tight-assed."

Kell slumped dramatically. "How did I know those words would come back to haunt me? You don't have to do this, Jamie."

"I know, but I want to. I want to act on what I'm feeling this moment." Her expression became animated. "Donna told me to quit thinking about everything and just *do.* I should bungee-jump off the Eiffel Tower if I want to or climb a skyscraper. Life is too short. I learned that over the weekend. You're here one minute and then you're gone. Can you understand that?"

Kell nodded. "I live that life, Jamie. Or at least, I did." It occurred to him then that Jamie's uncharacteristic behavior had to do with her father. It had to do about loss. He'd heard of this phenomenon...people who'd lost a loved one had a need to reaffirm the fact of their own existence by experiencing something edgy, thrilling...naughty! "But you won't be gone in the next minute, Jamie."

"How do you know?" She shifted her weight to one hip. A tough-girl stance. One that only made her more desirable, more thrilling. "You got any guarantees?"

"No," Kell said quietly. "I don't."

"Good. Then you're just like the rest of us mortals. Having no guarantees means you have to keep trying." With that, she reached around behind herself and unzipped her skirt. Then, with one supple move, the short skirt fell away...sliding down over her hips and pooling at her feet. Her blouse soon joined the skirt. "Take your clothes off, Commander. If you won't make love to me, then I'm going to make love to you."

He'd created a monster. Kell swallowed, watched her advance on him...smoothly, silkily, like a cat on the prowl. With her eyes narrowed, her chin up, she daringly tugged one bra strap down her arm, then the other. She reached around behind her again...and this time her bra came away. With two dainty fingers, she held it up—then dropped it to the floor. She grinned at him.

Kell didn't move. He couldn't. But she could and she did. She did a little shimmy that jiggled her bared breasts in such a way that made him ache. "Jamie." His voice was ragged, hoarse. "We can't do this here."

She stopped and eyed him in a teasing manner...while hooking her thumbs in the waistband of her lace panties. "What's the matter? Not...*up* for it?"

Kell exhaled sharply. "I'm plenty up for it." He was, too...uncomfortably so. Only a long-dead man wouldn't have been. "But this is nuts, Jamie." He indicated the room around them. "We're in your therapist's office."

She nodded. "Of course." She too examined the room with her slow-moving gaze that took in everything. "It's like one of the biggest fantasies around, you know. The therapist's couch. I mean, hello. I came in here to bare my soul to Dr. Hampton and talk about sex with you. So why not bare my body in here and *have* sex with you?"

Well, that made a hell of a lot of sensual sense. Who was he to fight it? Kell jumped up from the couch and began unbuttoning his shirt. "Okay. I'm in."

"Great." Jamie giggled and skipped toward him, helping him get out of all his clothes. "Took you long enough," she teased as she divested him of his pants. "You had me worried there for a moment. I thought I'd lost my attractiveness."

"Like hell," Kell assured her. He flung away his boxers. He was naked now...and proudly displaying the evidence of his intense desire for her. "Here. Let me help you," he said. Desire flared in her eyes, darkening them—and inflaming Kell.

He hooked his thumbs under the sheer material of her underwear and slowly slid them over Jamie's slender hips and down her firm thighs, all the while planting biting, nipping kisses across her exposed flesh. Jamie moaned and clutched at his hair, which only further incensed Kell's nerve endings. Quickly she stepped out of the lace and Kell tossed the last barrier aside. On his knees in front of her, he tugged her to him, kissed her flat belly all over and murmured, "Let me taste you, baby."

"Oh, God," Jamie groaned, going limp. Kell cupped his hands around her heart-shaped buttocks and held her steady...against his mouth. Instantly, expertly, he swirled his tongue around her crisp and curling dark hair until his attentions had it pushed aside. He nudged his tongue into the crevice that marked her womanhood and found her essence. With the tip of his tongue against the very nub of her desire...he paused, breathing in all his lungs could take of her woman's scent. A groan escaped him. He was on fire—and let her know it. Urgency gripped him as certainly as he gripped her bottom. His tongue performed its magic, opening her, making her wet, firing her senses...

"Oh, Kell...please. I can't..." Jamie's voice was deep, begging. Her knees were buckling. "I need you."

In one smooth motion, Kell was on his feet and was looking down into Jamie's face. Her eyelids drooped with desire but her gaze locked with his. She reached up to pull his head down to hers and kissed him with a wildness he'd never seen in Jamie before. He couldn't contain himself. Kell smoothed his hands over every delicious inch of her that he could reach. Jamie pushed herself against him in an unmistakable invitation...one that Kell answered. He lifted her up in his arms. Jamie wrapped her legs around his waist, and put her arms around his neck. Kell broke the kiss so he could see where they were—and where the couch was. In the next instant, he'd walked them over to it and was lowering them both down onto it with a crashing suddenness that left them both gasping.

In another instant, he was inside Jamie. Her slick wetness, her wonderful heat and tightness, closed around his length. He shuddered and thrust into her...over and over. He was unable even to be tender, but she didn't seem to mind. Jamie urged him on with whispered erotic words of blatant frankness that drove him wild. This was not making love. This was sex, pure and simple. It was an act that was a fulfillment of need. The sheer life force of need. And it carried them away. In all the world, there was only the two of them and their love that mattered.

UNTIL THEY STEPPED outside the treatment room and into Dr. Hampton's waiting room, that is. At least they were fully clothed, barely. Jamie's hair and makeup was a little mussed. Kell's shirt was buttoned wrong— but it was tucked in. They both looked guilty as hell...and as if they'd just done exactly what they'd just done. On Dr. Hampton's couch, no less.

At her desk, Roberta's chubby fingers stilled...but remained poised over her keyboard. She stared over her reading glasses at the couple standing in front of her. "Oh my," she said simply.

She turned to face her boss...who was—or had been until the door opened—leafing through a magazine. She and Kell met Dr. Hampton's knowing yet sober gaze. Thankfully, he was the only other occupant in the waiting room.

"Well," he said, this man who held her entire career in his hands, this man whose office sanctity she and Kell had just violated...along with about a handful of ethics. Dr. Hampton cleared his throat and put the magazine aside...and stared at them. And waited.

Kell nudged Jamie with his shoulder, hard enough to propel her forward a step. "Jamie has something she'd like to say."

She glared up at Kell, then focused on Dr. Hampton, trying not to see Roberta's shocked expression. "Dr. Hampton," Jamie began. "Kell and I...well, we have achieved closure."

"Ah." Dr. Hampton folded his hands together in his lap and crossed his legs. "I have to say that I, uh, thought as much."

The flames of acute embarrassment consumed Jamie's flesh. She wished she could melt right there on the spot. What had she been thinking? Of course Dr. Hampton and Roberta had to have known—and heard—what was going on inside that other room all this time.

"Dr. Hampton," Jamie began, "I suppose I've really done it now, haven't I? I wouldn't blame you if you reported me to the licensing bureau—"

"Hold on, Jamie. That reminds me."

Jamie exchanged a worried glance with Kell. They both watched as Dr. Hampton stood up and crossed over to Roberta. When he held his hand out, the secretary put a piece of paper into his hand. Then she gave him a pen. He signed the paper with a flourish and turned to Jamie, handing it to her. "Well done," he said, grinning. "You've earned this. And I don't mean by what you...just did. I mean by your fine work and your research. And by your efforts these past weeks to...well, you know, take care of things. I believe you when you say you have succeeded."

Baffled in the extreme, Jamie looked down at the paper Dr. Hampton had given her. Quickly she read it, Kell looking over her shoulder. Comprehension set in. She jerked around to face Kell. "Look—it's my license to practice. I'm certified." Tears formed in her eyes. "Ohmigod, I think I'm going to cry. Kell, I did it. *We* did it. We broke down the barriers, all the walls—and we became whole. I cannot believe this."

His face alight with joy, Kell swept her up in his arms and swung her around as Jamie laughed happily. When he put her down, he held her by the shoulders and stared down at her. "I am so proud of you, Jamie. I love you so much."

"I love you, too," she said, meaning every word wholeheartedly. She turned around in Kell's embrace and faced her mentor. All Jamie could do was stand there, clutching her license in her hands, and beam happily. "Thank you," she said. "This opens up a whole new world to me, Dr. Hampton. But more importantly, the person I love the most in all the world—" she smiled up at Kell "—will be sharing my life with me from this day on. He asked me again to marry him and I said yes."

"Oh!" Roberta plucked a tissue out of a box, took her glasses off and wiped at her eyes. "I just love a happy ending," she said, sniffling.

# ___Epilogue___

"IT WOULD HAVE BEEN fun to just jump on a plane and get married in Vegas. But it was better to have the ceremony here so our families, not to mention Jeff and Melanie, could be there, don't you think?" Sitting on the couch next to Kell, who held her hand, Jamie focused on Dr. Hampton.

Sitting in his usual chair, Dr. Hampton nodded. "Oh, I do. It was a wonderful gesture. I'd never been on a military base. The Camdens' quarters were beautifully decorated for your wedding."

"I'll say," Kell answered. "Melanie is quite the woman. She did it all herself, even though she's pregnant. Well, she says Jeff helped. But I'm sure she didn't let him do much since he's still recuperating."

"I'm so glad he's doing well. Now, tell me, how is married life treating you? It's been three months now."

A little misty, Jamie answered. "I love it. It's so great just to be old married folks. He leaves for the office every morning, comes home every evening. I'm there working at home and looking forward all day to seeing him come through the door. It couldn't be any better, Dr. Hampton." Jamie tucked her hair behind her ears. "Have I ever thanked you for making me seek closure?"

Dr. Hampton chuckled. "About a hundred times. Again...you're welcome."

Jamie smoothed her hands over the couch's firm cushions...and locked gazes with Kell. His face colored along with hers. Jamie cleared her throat and looked Dr. Hampton's way. "I like your new couch." She could barely make herself meet the man's gaze. "And it was, uh, really nice of you to give us your *other* one for a wedding gift."

Dr. Hampton's eyes lit with humor. "It seemed like an appropriate gesture...given the circumstances, wouldn't you say?"

"I would," Jamie quickly agreed. "But seriously, Dr. Hampton, we owe you a huge debt. How can we ever repay you?"

He brushed away her gratitude. "Oh, please, I just did my job. But who knows? If you ever write a book...dedicate it to me, okay?"

Jamie exchanged a charged glance with Kell. A twinkle lit her eyes. She thought of her big secret—the completed manuscript she'd just turned in two days ago to Highline Publishing. "No problem."

# Pamela Burford presents

## The Wedding Ring

***Four high school friends and a pact—
every girl gets her ideal mate by thirty or be
prepared for matchmaking! The rules are
simple. Give your "chosen" man three
months...and see what happens!***

### Love's Funny That Way
*Temptation #812*—on sale December 2000
It's no joke when Raven Muldoon falls in love with comedy
club owner Hunter—*brother* of her "intended."

### I Do, But Here's the Catch
*Temptation #816*—on sale January 2001
Charli Ross is more than willing to give up her status as
last of a dying breed—the thirty-year-old virgin—to Grant.
But all *he* wants is marriage.

### One Eager Bride To Go
*Temptation #820*—on sale February 2001
Sunny Bleecker is still waiting tables at Wafflemania when
Kirk comes home from California and wants to marry her.
It's as if all her dreams have finally come true—except...

### Fiancé for Hire
*Temptation #824*—on sale March 2001
No way is Amanda Coppersmith going to let
The Wedding Ring rope her into marriage. But no matter
how clever she is, Nick is one step ahead of her...

***"Pamela Burford creates the
memorable characters readers love!"***
***—The Literary Times***

**#1** *New York Times* bestselling author

# NORA ROBERTS

brings you more of the loyal and loving,
tempestuous and tantalizing Stanislaski family.

*Coming in February 2001*

# The Stanislaski Sisters

### Natasha and Rachel

Though raised in the Old World traditions of their
family, fiery Natasha Stanislaski and cool, classy
Rachel Stanislaski are ready for a *new* world of love....

*And also available in February 2001 from
Silhouette Special Edition, the newest book in the
heartwarming Stanislaski saga*

# CONSIDERING KATE

Natasha and Spencer Kimball's daughter Kate turns her
back on old dreams and returns to her hometown, where
she finds the *man* of her dreams.

*Available at your favorite retail outlet.*

*Silhouette* ®

*Where love comes alive*™

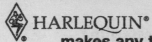

From bestselling
Harlequin American Romance author

# CATHY GILLEN THACKER

comes

# TEXAS VOWS

## A McCABE FAMILY SAGA

Sam McCabe had vowed to always
do right by his five boys—but after
the loss of his wife, he needed the small-town security
of his hometown, Laramie, Texas, to live up to that
commitment. Except, coming home would bring him
back to a woman he'd sworn to stay away from.
It will be one vow that Sam can't keep....

On sale March 2001

Available at your favorite retail outlet.

HARLEQUIN®
*Makes any time special* ™